CW00860284

GIVE A LITTLE BIT

WHEN ARE YOU COMING BACK?

PAM CROFT

Order this book online at www.trafford.com
or email orders@trafford.com

Most Trafford titles are also available at major online book retailers.

Print information available on the last page.

ISBN: 978-1-4907-9402-0 (sc)
ISBN: 978-1-4907-9403-7 (hc)
ISBN: 978-1-4907-9404-4 (e)

Library of Congress Control Number: 2019936112

Trafford rev. 03/04/2019

 www.trafford.com
North America & international
toll-free: 1 888 232 4444 (USA & Canada)
fax: 812 355 4082

Yes, I think I have a very interesting story to tell. Whether you choose to believe it or not it's totally up to you!

I shall begin with fictional characters so I may protect myself from future attacks of others.

Time of launch here would be 1973.

There once was a girl who was quite the tomboy and having a wonderful childhood. Her name was Sue and she will be telling this story. She had many dreams, of course, just like anyone else. She loved basketball so much her father built her an outdoor court on the back of the garage in the alley. It came to be known every Sunday afternoon, the neighborhood boys would come challenge her. Either a game of horse or around the world or a little bit of one-on-one with touchable fouls that were fun! Too bad, she was good, and the boys would always say home-court advantage. Another category she is still known for is when her boyfriend would ride his bike over to the house. I would say when she was fourteen with his ten-speed orange bike was when this occurred. Sure enough, she wanted one so badly just like his. Freedom 10 was the brand. She begged and begged her father for one. So eventually, her parents gave in and bought one for her and her brother. Hers was white, and his was yellow. It was so amazing to be able to ride anywhere. Unfortunately, her brother

1

was rather big, and his foot got caught on the pavement, and a huge wreck occurred with a skull fracture. He is smarter because of this. She, however, saw her boyfriend popping wheelies with his bike one day and said, "Teach me how to do this." After weeks of practice, she accomplished this task. Turns out, she could out wheelie any boy on the street in distance. They accepted it quite well. Later on in life, about forty years, I would say a person looked at her in a store and said, "Hi, wheelie girl!" She was shocked. He remembered watching her practice in the street all day.

Another thing she and her brother were known for was loud music playing in the summer in their house. When their mother would go to the store, they would go straight to the console and put some forty-fives on and rock out. No complaints though. The most memorable one was Abba's "Waterloo." We would crank it up so loud people walking by would smile and clap. She loves this song so much to this day.

She played sports with great enthusiasm. Unfortunately, her coaches were more interested in her than how she could play the sport!

She received a lot of mail on being a stewardess. Unfortunately, her teeth were crooked.

She took a lot of business courses, which allowed her to type, shorthand, and do accounting. This eventually helped her with her first jobs. This is important in this story.

One thing she thoroughly enjoyed with her father was to watch war movies with him. This too is important in this story. Her father was in the military and wanted her to see how important the armed forces were in past wars. She found this very exciting but realized women in the military was not common.

So as her life continued onward, she graduated high school, not with flying colors, and set out for the real world.

She had some men trouble, mainly dealing with her mother's wishes that did not happen. Her first real job was being a secretary for a vice president of manufacturing and engineering at a local glass plant. She absolutely loved it, even her own parking place.

She had her own apartment and car! Unfortunately, the job soon was to end because of the economy, and she was laid off.

She tried and tried to find any employment. After four months of trying and trying, she was pretty depressed as to what she was going to do.

She decided to write the governor of her state to see what she was doing wrong with the unemployment department that was supposed to help her find a job. Every time she went in there, they did not help her. She was not allowed to move back home because of her mother and her wishes.

Lo and behold, she did get a response from the governor! He wrote back that a team of people would be coming to see what the problem was and try to help her.

So that day came, and the team of people came as well. She had to dress up and present herself in a way that she never had to before. She was very, very nervous. The meeting went very well. The team of people asked many questions about her work ethics. She told them no one was a harder worker than her and she was willing to learn anything because she had a car and apartment payment. She really wanted to stay in office work where she knew office skills. However, at this point, anything would work.

They took many notes, and at the end of the meeting, they concluded that she was not treated fairly and would get an apology from the workers that day. They also asked her if she was willing to work anywhere the next time something came up even if it was not office work. She agreed to this very happily and told them yes. She left there very happy that day and more confident than ever.

It probably was about a week later she went back down to the unemployment building to check things, and sure enough, the same not-so-nice woman looked at her with a snarly smile and said, "I have a job opening just for you, and you are sure to get it."

Now remember I agreed to any type of job.

I was so excited and nervous at the same time. I asked where and when do I go for the interview. She said tomorrow would be fine and it was at a local department discount store. There were two openings, one for the office and one as a cashier. I said great and instantly thought now I have an office job again. She told me to call a number and ask for a man who was the manager to set up the interview. I said thank you, and she snarled again and said "you're welcome and good luck" with a weird tone to her voice. At that point, I asked, "Where is this?" She replied the name of the store, and I really did not know much about it. My mother had taken me there as a child, but that was all I remembered. My mother came to my apartment a few days later and said I needed to call this store for an interview. I left my apartment and drove straight to my mother's house to use her phone to call. When I got there, my parents were both there and asked my where my interview would be. I, at that point, have never seen such expressions on their faces. First, they said, "Oh no." Then they said this might not work out. Then they asked me if I know the owner. Then they asked how tough I am. I was thinking to myself, *Pretty damn tough for what you have put me through with lately.* So I asked what the problem with this place was.

They told me that most people could not work there very long because the owner was so mean and bullied you as you work. He would watch you and follow you every day, along with yelling at you. My mother said, "Don't you remember when you were little and I told you not to touch anything because the owner would yell at you when we shopped there?" I did not remember any of this. I was not really worried because I thought I am going to be in the office anyway, so he wouldn't be in there.

Now my father did say he had the upmost respect with him and that he never ever gave him problems when he shops there. It was at this point they told me that he was a Holocaust survivor and started in a tent. I did not know what to say to this as I did not know then how devastating that was in his life. I just could not grasp that at that point. All I wanted was a job. They also knew I agreed to the governor's staff that I would take whatever job came available after our meeting. I reminded them of this, and they just shrugged and said good luck with that same weird tone as the woman at the unemployment building.

So I picked up the phone and placed my call. My interview was the following day, and not so eagerly did I await its arrival.

PAM CROFT

Pumping myself up for an easy interview in this not so great place was all I did to prepare for this. I was sure the office job would work for a while until something better came along. When I walked in, I saw cashiers in ugly smocks and busily working. I asked for the manager and told them I was there for an interview. She said, "Oh, let me get Mr. So-and-So," because the manager was not there.

Well, Mr. So-and-So was the person everyone had been telling me about. I looked at him with his business proprietor attitude and said, "Yes, I am here for the interview." He took me down to the end of the building, while everyone stared, and stopped at the layaway desk. He asked me my credentials with leery eyes. He asked me what happened at my last job. He said there was a cashier opening. I replied I thought there was an office one as well. He said yes, but for me, the cashier one would be best. Shockingly, I did not know what to say, except I had never run a register before. However, office work, I knew. He proceeded with the interview as if not to care.

He asked me, as I say, the million-dollar question, which I later learn was everyone's question, "What is 12 x 12?"

I was baffled. One, because I am the worst at math. Two, because I knew this was important for the cashier's job. Three, how can I delay this answer?

So I plainly said, "Can I tell you at the end of the interview?"

He just looked at me and went on with the interview, asking where I grew up and had I ever been in trouble with the law.

Meanwhile, I was determined to get this stupid math question answered in my head, I quickly did 10 x 12 and somehow added the rest.

So he was definitely done with this interview and said we could walk to the door. As we were walking to the door, he was telling me, "Thank you for coming in," and I blurted out, "144!" He asked what was 144. I said, "12 x 12," hoping it was the right answer.

He smiled and said, "Well, you did get it right."

I smiled because I was so proud of myself, not caring what he thinks, and I said thank you and left, hoping they do not call me back.

So could you imagine what happened next? Of course, I got the call. I called them back from my parents' house.

"Hey, Pam, this is the store calling, and you have the job. It will be a cashier position, and we would like you to start in two days, if possible." As my heart raced and nausea set in, I realized I had to take this job because of my wonderful governor and what he did for me. So I accepted with a not so exciting sound in my voice and tried to say a good "thank you" to the manager.

My mother and father said, "How nice," with some hesitation in their voices.

My mother said, "That is not what you studied in high school. You were supposed to be in an office."

I looked at her and let her know she is so right, like I already did not know this. Little did I know cashiering would be harder than I ever imagined.

So two days came, and I was finally off to work again. Yeah, sure enough, as I learn this job, the people from the unemployment office were coming in, pretending to need an item just so they could go through my line and give me a smirk.

When I got to my job the first day, I remember receiving a beautiful polyester gold smock you are required to wear during your shift. YUCK! Next, a name tag, which I followed them into the office to get. There, I thought I should be in here not out there. Next would be introducing me to all the other workers. We got back out on the floor, and lo and behold, there was the owner coming in. I did not know whether to feel proud to have gotten the job or the math question right when I saw him. I was sure it was the math question. He said "good morning" with a smile. I just said hi and noticed everyone ran like mice to look busy. A very nervous environment had arrived.

As the manager took me around the store, there was no way I would ever remember all these names. I just smiled again and acted like I was so happy to be there, thinking not much longer for my office job I would apply for elsewhere.

Next came the morning duties of cleaning, newspaper for the windows now, gets them real clean, and then your hands are black, so watch what you touch when you are done. Dust bunnies under racks are needed to be gotten as well. Whaaat? This is crazy. Next, straighten the shelves and make sure all jackets are zipped and facing the front of store. Whaaat? This is bad. Wrap the hangers with tape and get all returns ready from the night before. How about those carts? If they are wet, dry them off so they do not rust. OK, I can understand this one.

So after getting the hang of all this, I needed to learn how to run a register.

It was a time when digital registers were arriving, and this fine store was updating theirs. The most important thing to remember were the department numbers. I did not quite understand the reasoning behind it, but I said, "Sure, I will learn them," when really, I knew I was not.

You had to, of course, count your drawer in first thing. Since I had never worked with money before, this task took me about fifteen minutes to conquer. Everyone else was up and running, while I still was trying to get it to come out right. Did anyone feel sorry for me? No, they just went on their way, and then I figured out why they did not show me a faster way.

The owner always came through about fifteen minutes after opening, so lo and behold, what was I still doing? This only made me more nervous, so I acted like all was good and threw the money in and started working as I greeted the owner walking by. This could be the reason my drawer was not right sometimes.

As I had a trainer to help at first, they kept trying to let me be on my own, which took forever.

The departments were ganging up on me, only to hear "Wrong department again, wrong department again," then finally, "TAKE THIS HOME AND STUDY THE SHEET ON DEPARTMENTS!"

So as much as I did not care, I did. It seemed to me every day got worse, and my drawer would never ever come out. This would start each morning with trying to wait on a customer while the older evil office manager would fly out from behind the wall, only to come to me yelling, "What is wrong with you?" and "Why isn't your drawer right again?"

After my customer left, she would still be standing there with papers in her hand. I really needed this job after all, so I would say, "I have no idea what happened again."

Then she said, "Everything was being rang up on one department all day. How can we sell only clothing all day long?"

Many times this happened. Finally, the owner came out on a bright morning day, and I knew I wished I had an evening shift. The owner only showed up briefly at night, after dinner, usually happy.

So on this morning, he strolled over to me and said, "Take a walk with me."

This either meant maybe office work or bad cashier. Of course, it was bad cashier. He said that I had been here a month and was not doing good at all. What is wrong with me? I said I did not know and that I had never been a cashier before I knew office work. He said he was very disappointed in me, and the only thing he could do was give me a few more tries, and if it did not get better, he would let me go. He was tired of losing money with me.

He said I did not know how to even greet the customers right or sack things right either. I thought I was going to be sick because I still needed this job and did not want the unemployment place laughing at me. I wanted to win this.

After my shift that day, I went over to my mother's house and cried to her about this situation. She was quite upset with me for not knowing how to handle money. So she sat me down, and for the next five hours, I did cash register time. Little did I know there was a way to count back change. My brother visited that day also and, with him being a middle school math teacher, was totally amazed at my lack of knowledge.

I must add to this story by saying that in the sixth grade, I was having trouble keeping up with the math thing, so I raised my hand and asked my teacher if she could slow up a bit, and she said, "If you can't keep up with this, go get a tutor. I am not going to change my pace for you." Yes, in front of everyone, so I never asked a math question again and did poorly in this subject.

Now then, my brother came to the conclusion that the register always showed what change should be given back at the end of the transaction. This was true, so he said, "Why in the world would you not look at it twice to make sure what you are giving them is right?" WOW! It works.

My drawer slowly got better and better. Maybe this job will work out.

So as the days moved onward, my job duties increased with this. Besides learning how to talk to the customers because, as it was drilled into my head by the owner, "they are your bread and butter," I actually started to like this weird class of people that were coming in to shop. I will get to the customer base later on in this story.

My duties, however, increased to the Monday morning write up of what was to be transferred to the stores down south. Yes, he had two more stores that needed merchandise once a week. Now to do this, it got me away from the front of the store. Yeah! We would go out to lawn and garden to do this. There were pens that we would have to write down every box that was in them. I did not realize, however, this would include the departments they were from. Uh oh, hope I picked the right one. How many times I was told about this. Then the weather got colder, and oh my, how you would freeze out there! You were on a time limit also to get the merchandise on the truck to go down. Of course, if the owner thought it should be done by now, he would walk all the way back to quietly see if you were working and what the problem was. "Just finishing up," we would say. Then we would have a good cuss session after he went back up front. Week by week, I did get faster at this, and he actually liked me doing this job. So somehow I started to feel important at this crazy job.

The employees liked me, and it was starting to be fun.

During this time, my ex-boyfriend convinced me to come to Virginia to live and try it again. I thought, *Well, I am young and maybe this is what I should try to do.* So I gave my notice, and I did not think the owner was all that happy. On my last day, I went up to him and shook his hand. I told him it was a pleasure to work there even if I was a not so good cashier. He smiled at me and wished me the best of luck. *That* was a major thing for him to say. I could not believe it. He normally would look at people leaving, letting them believe no other place would be better than his. So off I went to Virginia, never to return to this job ever.

I think it was a three-month tour away. I lay on the beach every day and enjoyed it. My parents came to see me. I had a job at a grocery store nearby, as a cashier, of course. It is too bad I never showed up for it. I knew, by this time, that I did not want to stay in Virginia. There were people I was missing more than I thought I would. I also knew this relationship was not good like you picture it might be.

I came back to Ohio after three months. I moved back in to my parents' home. They seemed happy because they thought I was still with my ex and they loved him. I knew I was not going to be with him. When it came time to find work, my parents asked if I could go back to the store I had left. I hesitated because I really was a bit scared to go back. I did not want to look like a failure for one thing. After a long thought, I told them it was a possibility. My loving dad shopped there every Sunday. He came back one Sunday and said that they were ready for me to just call. He told them I was back in town. Well, this would be the second time to go back if I went. I think the total would be five when this book finishes. I hope you will continue to read.

I got the nerve up to call and talk to the manager. He sounded happy I was back and said there was an opening for me if I wanted it. Yes, it was a cashier job. I started back very nervous, but I received a very warm welcome, and everyone loved my tan. Then the owner came in and looked amazed to see me there at my register. I just smiled and said, "Don't ask," and I was happy to be back. He smirked a nice smile and said, "I hope you are better than last time."

I never realized the customer liked me until I came back. They said "welcome back" when they approached my register. Wow, really starting to like this retail stuff.

PARKING LOT SALE

As I worked at my second time around, we did a lot fun things. During the summers, it was very important to have our annual outdoor parking lot sale. This sale was not only important because we're getting rid of old, lost merchandise, but also so I could get a great suntan working it!

There I am, hoping I would get picked to go outdoors for the day. Surely not very many people come to this stupid event. Well, I did get picked. I had to be there extra early to help move items out. Yeah! No ugly smock to wear that day. You are allowed to wear shorts and tank tops.

So there I am, all proud, when I noticed tons and tons of people pulling into the parking lot. All of a sudden, a bad memory came back to me. When I was little, my mom dragged me down there to shop in the hot, hot blacktop heat of summer to look for a pair of shoes. I thought my shoes were going to melt on this surface and could not wait to leave. Oh well, too late now. Here I am, ready to do this.

As I was saying, the people were coming in one by one by one. All of them were shouting.

"Where is the shoe special you advertised?"

"Where is the shaving cream you said you have?"

"When can I get a better color towel than this?"

"Are the same specials inside the store?"

Then the head cashier asked me if I knew the special. "Sure," I said, not really knowing. We had two registers that day, and the line went forever. I was messing up bad, so I pleaded to just let me bag items. That worked, and the day went so fast, so fast I forgot to check my sunburn that was slowly creeping up on me. Yes, worst burn ever! I never said a word and just kept working. It was quite fun. I noticed one of my managers was getting happier as the day went on. How can he be so happy? Then I realized he kept running to the other warehouse often. So maybe there was some extra good lemonade there I do not know, but whatever the reason is, I did not care if he was a fun person.

After lugging things back inside of the store, my shift was over. The owner thanked me for my work that day, and I said it was really fun. He commented how tan I had become and to be careful with that. Well, the next day, I went to work in a tank top also because my shoulder was so burned I could not wear the stupid smock I was supposed to wear. That morning, the owner came in as I was counting my drawer. It was Sunday, and he was always in a good mood that day. He took one look at me, and I thought, *Oh no, I am in trouble for no smock.* He came right up to me and looked at my blistered shoulders and said, "Come with me." I followed him nervously to the first-aid aisle, and he took a tube of cream off the shelf and said, "Put this on and keep it with you. You are badly burned, and I feel bad for you." Can you believe this? Not only was I shocked, but also, I now viewed the owner in a whole new way.

As I was gaining confidence in the retail world, my personal life was a little crazy. I was still living with my parents when one person I was missing called their house. The reason he called was his friend had come through my line at work and said he did not know I had moved back. So he told the person I was missing, and he had missed me too. Now my parents did not like this man at all. He was a little older and was not their pick for me. When he called their house, he wanted to see me. So I met him, and it was then I wanted to spend the rest of my life with him. When I got back to my parents, they told me if I was going to see him, I would have to move out. So I told him, and he said, "Great! That means we will get married!" So I had not moved in with him until the marriage.

We married in the summer, about two months later. We eloped to West Virginia, and I went back to work two days later. Everyone was quiet to me when I clocked in. They did not know what to say. Questions were asked if I did really get married. "Good luck" was a lot of response to me.

So as my work life continued still at this store, it became more and more interesting. I was starting to understand the owner's moods. One moment, he would be happy and corresponding with the customers; the next, when they left, he would want to make sure everyone was working. When he would walk out on the floor to the coats, you better hope someone went through them that morning to make sure they were all buttoned and zipped properly, sale tag facing outward, and no—I mean NO—hangers empty on the rack. So as I pretended I was busy dusting or straightening and at a good distance from him, sure enough, the hanger angrily made its way through the air to the registers, avoiding hitting any person.

He had his way with boisterous words with the manager. Never once did he call you by name. It was always "dingy," "Susie," or "you." You have to remember it is still the early eighties, so all this was OK. I understood to not get in trouble was to keep busy. Then again, if I was paying people, they would not stand around either. My respect for the owner was starting to happen. We also had softball games on Sundays, which was fun. They used to have a bowling team, I learned also.

I was learning about his life before this store.

He was a Holocaust survivor. No one else in his family survived. He had been in five camps. He was a cement laborer and other things not so good either. He had big family too. He had aunts and uncles and cousins who were here in the United States. His father never thought it was going to get bad, so he stayed back. Never did he see them again once taken. How horrible. I saw the numbers on his arm every day. My emotional respect was growing and growing. He found his relatives here in the United States after the war.

He knew he wanted to start a business, so he found an area that reminded him of Europe and put up a huge tent alongside a highway and sold items from it. He was there day in and day out. Hot or cold weather, it did not matter, he was there. He had squatter's rights and soon was going to build a store there. He lived up on a hill in a log cabin.

There were great stories from that tent. My customers always talked about the tent. In the winter, he had some beverages to warm you up also. I have seen pictures of this tent, and it was amazing.

So after the tent, he built his first store. It did fantastic. He met his wife also. She was going to nursing school and needed a job. She never worked as a nurse but became a solid fixture in his life. The log cabin became a beautiful home too. One day a skunk had gotten into the log home, and bad things happened. So they spent the next month at a hotel while the new house was built.

Soon the new store did so well, a bigger and better one was built next to it. Now he had two stores and still growing. More expansion was on his mind: shoe stores downtown, start a store thirty miles away, and maybe one more twelve miles away. He had more stores in the first store, along with a barbershop. He built more buildings with gyms and photo-taking stores. He had beauty salons renting from him. It was crazy! Then I learned he had made the Fortune 500 list back in the seventies! What the—?

So while I am watching this man at his biggest years, enjoying the peanuts we warmed up in the mornings to sell, watching the big salesmen swinging through the doors with their brief cases and merchandise, him making them wait at least fifteen minutes before popping out of his office, them being so thirsty for a sale trying to understand his sharp mind—yes, I was loving this—he must have noticed me staring one day at his performance with a nervous, sweaty salesman. He looked at me and said, "What do you think, dingy?" I thought I was going to faint. I tried to say it all looks good, then went out on the floor. Wow, did he really want my opinion? I felt so good from this little stupid thing.

Well, I became pregnant and knew I wanted to be a stay-at-home mother. This did not go so well with him. Back then, bosses did not like women to get pregnant because they knew they would have to leave. So I told him, after my baby goes to school, I might be back. Anger was in his face. He did not talk to me much after that.

I had a beautiful baby boy. One of my managers gave me a shower from the store. It was about two years later, I was eating at a restraint with my family, and I saw the owner there. I became very nervous but told my husband I wanted to go say hi. I took my son over to meet him. He was reading the paper and looked up at me and smiled. He gave my son a dime and asked me when I was coming back. I just stared in disbelief. I said, "I did not think you thought I was that good of a worker."

He shrugged and said, "Just wondering."

I said I couldn't until my son goes to school. He said fine and went back to reading his paper.

I felt good about seeing him. My mom and I started going to bingo on Monday nights. I didn't know when I decided this, but soon I was stopping into the store before bingo to say hi to the owner. The first time I did, I didn't know he was in a bad mood, and when he was in a bad mood, you stayed away. The manager said that I better not go into his office and say hi. I just said it would be OK and went on. I knocked, and he said, "Come in," not even looking up from his paper.

I said, "Hello there," and he said, "What the hell do you want?"

I said I just wanted to say hi but wouldn't bother him again. I left very hurt.

The manager said, "I told you."

That night I told my husband about this, and he said I should not have gone in. A couple of weeks later, my husband went in to the store to buy something and saw the owner. The owner came up to him and asked how I was and what I wanted the other week I came in. My husband said I wanted nothing but to say hi to him and that was the kind of person I was when I like someone. The owner said I caught him off guard that day and to tell me hi.

Well, I waited a few weeks and said I would never go back in there when—what did I do? Yes, I went back in to say hi to everyone and him. He treated me the best ever and offered me bingo money for the night. I said no but would be back to say hi again. He teased me and said, "I know you will."

As the years progressed and the question was always "when are you coming back," our relationship was, in a weird way, growing. The employees would look at me when I would come in and say, "He really does like you," but why? People would ask me, "Why do you visit this guy who is not very nice?" I don't know if it was because my last name might have been in the same background as him or the fact that he knew my grandfather and my father well. My grandfather's name was the same as his brother's. There was a connection that I could not explain. I did not care if people thought I was weird talking to him.

I became pregnant just as soon as my son was to start school. This put a bad feeling on my visits to the store because he was sure I would soon return after the school year was started. When I told him I was pregnant again, he was upset. He said congratulations and went into his office. I didn't know why he never had children, and I felt bad for this. After that, he would dodge into his office every time I came to visit. So I never went in. I said to tell him hi.

I had a second beautiful son. I was going to stay home for five more years and then maybe go back to work. My first son was very calm. The second son was totally opposite. After one year of a rowdy, energetic, screaming child, I said to my husband I might not make it five years with no work. I felt like I needed to get out of the house and go back to work. He didn't quite understand but would soon know what I was talking about. I went and visited one day with my second son, and the owner was out front. I went right up to him and said, "Here he is." I held him out and made him hold him. He laughed and held him at arm's length. I said, "Wow, what a way to hold a baby!" Everyone could not believe I did that. I loved it.

Then he asked, "When are you coming back?"

I asked my manager if I could come back. Where else was I going to go at this point of my life and it was close to home? The manager said he would have to talk to the owner. I said fine. A couple of days later, of course, I had my job back. Everything was great. Most employees welcomed me back. Some just stared as if to say, "Here she goes again." The new head cashier was just like a mom. The owner's name for her was Granny. She did not mind that and always had yummy food for us to eat that was homemade. Later I learned our birthdays were the same. So as I was happy to be back, one of the managers was a little sour on me. My schedule was not the best at times. She was in charge of this. The owner would yell out her name from the front of the store if he could not find her. All the customers would be alarmed at his voice. Our shelves were always to be low. Nothing higher than four feet so that the owner could see everyone, which made it hard to goof off at any time. Smart, right?

Sundays were still the owner's best mood day. My dad would always come in to buy something that day just to see me, I think. The owner was very funny about family visiting, and this made me very nervous. He surely was not allowed to come through my line. I had told him this *soooo* many times before.

One Sunday, he came in and said hi to the owner, who was always out front to see customers. Sure enough, my father went up to the owner and said, "She's all yours now," pointing at me, laughing. I tried not to look at them but couldn't help it, and both of them were laughing like they were good friends! So I accepted my dad's visits more openly on Sundays from that point on. He still tried to come through my line that day, and I said, "No, no, no."

I did not appreciate how badly the manager were afraid of the owner. If I had a question about pricing an item and was asking them and the owner would come out of his office, the manager would turn and walk away from me like a scared puppy, leaving me stranded alone, looking stupid at the owner. One day, when the owner told me to do something and I was working on something the manager had told me to do, I learned to do what the owner wants done first after getting told so by the owner. I made a decision to not ever run away if he came out of his office. What is there to be scared of? Getting yelled at? Never would I run away like my managers would.

On Sundays, the owner would walk around the store to make sure things were in order and shelves were stocked. He would ask a cashier to walk with him, and they dreaded this. For some strange reason, I could not wait for my turn. I was going to have fun if I got motioned to go on THE WALK. So when it finally happened, I just smiled. He took me to the drug aisle and pointed at some shampoo that was not pulled forward. I must have been very nervous because I blurted out, "UH OH!" He cracked up laughing and said, "What was that? Uh oh?" He called me "uh oh" the rest of the day. He loved to take little kids to the candy aisle and let them pick something out. Although they looked scared at first, they would be happy in the end. My mother always told me to not touch anything when we would shop there when I was little because the owner would not like it and yell. I never got offered the free candy. Boo.

During Christmas, he was in such a good mood. It meant more money for one thing. He had a wrapping station in the back of the store so people could get their presents wrapped before leaving. It was the new thing for classiness. Well, sure enough again, the owner came up to me and said, "Go down there and wrap some presents." I was, and still am, the worst wrapper ever. After about three items, he said, "Where did you learn this method? Go back to your register," shaking his head.

He would give out Christmas candy to the customers as well. They loved it—boxes and boxes of chocolate- covered cherries. He really liked holidays, which is why he wanted to be open for most of them. He gave us turkeys one year. He would give us candy also, along with something special in our checks. One year he tricked us into thinking $20 was our bonus. He said, if our efforts got better within the month, there might be more. We all were pretty mad, but he did give us a lot more at Christmas. His birthday was on Christmas Eve. Being Jewish, I told him he really was Jesus Christ. He did not laugh at this but more of gave an eye-roll. Christmas was a special time in there.

Pricing items was an issue also but fun. He always taught you to put the price in the upper-right-hand corner of the product; anything else was wrong. So as I was pricing so proudly, sure enough again, he sent the yellow sticker—that all of Lancaster knew—to another area of the product for some reason or another. What a challenge, and I was so happy when he would say "good job." If it was not a good job, peel them all off and start over. Yeah!

When relatives were coming to town, it was major cleaning and straightening for days. Excitement for us around the corner. There was little lady aunt from New York. Filling her cart up with merchandise was a must from him. "Fuller," he would say, then would take it to his car. He loved her so much. Cousins were a little trickier, who was who. There was some from California, some from New York, some from Georgia, and some from Washington.

So as my schedule worsened, there was this billboard issue I must tell you about. The owner advertised very much. I think he had at least four billboards around town that were his. Being from Europe, he believed in pretty woman in sexy clothes. He posted this billboard advertising the store with a beautiful woman with a very sexy top on. It showed a little cleavage even. He got a call from the Lancaster committee about people complaining about this woman and her cleavage. He said, "So what?"

A week later, they called back and said, "You must take this picture down. It is offending the city."

He was so mad. Everyone, at this point, was out to find this billboard to see this bad picture. The town was talking about it all the time. When I saw it, I did not understand the problem. Some religious groups were also upset with this billboard. Well, he took it down to please the city.

He always carried his camera with him. He was quite good at photography. A few years after the billboard incident, he was traveling down the road in front of his store. He came upon a new picture on the billboard. Lo and behold, it was a woman lying in the sand in a string bikini advertising beer. He went nuts. He pulled over and got his camera out and took a picture of this sexy woman smiling at him. I found this picture years later in a pile up at his house. I do not know if he protested it. I am pretty sure he called about this billboard, but nothing ever happened, and it stayed up a very long time.

By this time, there was a grocery store in his first store, a bakery, a barbershop, and a gym across the way. His little plaza was booming. It was such fun to get a break at work and go get a chocolate milk and one of the best doughnuts ever. I became good friends with the barber. He was there quite a while, but just like always, the owner would fight with the renters, and they would leave. I just could not understand why these fights would happen, and it made me sad. During this time, I need to tell you my mother and I made up, and she would visit me as well at work. More on that later.

It was so much fun to watch everyone scramble when he would fly through the front doors unannounced, especially when we thought he was on a trip. So relaxed we were until the headlight would shine through the front doors, and sure enough, he's back! If good things happened on the trip, he was OK at first, but if it was a bad trip, do not try to talk to him. You would know in an instant which way it went. A new suit specified a good trip. Before his trips, he would pick at everything in the store. He wanted you to be busy at all times, or else . . . That was a dead giveaway that he would be going on a trip. "What day" was the only question, with "please let it be tomorrow." We also learned the Jewish holidays very well and even felt like we were also a little Jewish ourselves. His moods would reflect the holiday.

My schedule was getting worse and worse, night shifts then came the awful split shifts, nine to one then go home and come back from five to nine. What about my family? My son was playing sports at this time, so what about seeing his game? Nope. So once again, it was time to leave. So I did.

Whenever I would go into the store to buy something, the owner would once again run into his office to avoid me. After a year of this, I was really wanting to talk to him.

I was still going out with the people I worked with. We would go have some drinks and dance so I could get out of the house. Well, one night I had a few too many, like many do, and thought, wow, I really would love to talk and see him since he was not getting any younger. People always said what a tyrant he was, but I always disagreed, even though we had our fights. So as I was on my way home, I looked up the hill at his house behind the store. I saw a bunch of lights on. So I went right up the long winding driveway to this man's castle on the hill. I got out of my car and rang the doorbell. No answer. I rang it several more times. Finally, the garage door opened slowly, and as I peeked under it, there he was with a ball bat in his hand. I jumped back and said, "Hi there."

He said, "Hunny, what are you doing? What is wrong?"

I said, "I wanted to talk to you, and you always run away from me at the store." I asked quickly, "If I come to the store, will you talk to me and not run away?"

He said yes and told me to go home. I said, "Great," and left. I felt victorious.

The next day, I did not feel so well and soon realized what I had done. I did not tell anyone. I waited a week until I went into the store. The owner was in his office. The manager came up to me and said hi. Then he asked, "Did you go up to his house last week?"

I said, "Yes, why?"

"The owner said you did and that you wanted something, but he did not know what." The manager said, "That was pretty brave of you."

Just then, the owner came out, and for sure I thought he would go back in his office, but guess what, he came right up to me and said, "Are you all right?"

I said, "Yes. I just want to talk to you sometimes when I come in."

He said, "Fine, and when are you coming back?"

I laughed and said soon.

So moving on with this wonderful story, I hope you are enjoying it, there is a lot left to read that will just make you smile and hopefully feel what I lived.

During this time, I was still debating on whether I should return again or just enjoy life. The movies and TV shows were starting to talk more and more about the Holocaust era. I was really starting to watch it more and more. Just knowing someone that had gotten through this horrific ordeal—not just one camp but five of them—was really pulling at my heart strings. I also was understanding his way of running his business. I came to find out he actually helped build his buildings and laid the block. He did not like the way some of the workers were doing it, so he thought he would just do it himself since that is what kept him alive in the camps. I came to the conclusion that I was missing learning more about this man and his business. I also was missing retail and the way people would purchase items. I was missing the people as well.

I slowly told my husband one day that I was wanting to go back to the store and work. He just shrugged and said, "Good luck, and how long this time? You cannot keep doing this—go back and then quit."

I said, "Well, I can't help it." The owner makes me so mad at times.

He said, "Do whatever you want."

I went into the store and went to the manager who worked there since high school and nicely asked if I could come back again. He was not too happy about this but said he would ask the owner and let me know. Yeah! I got the call to come back. Now remember, this store has employed about everyone in town, but turnover is a lot because of the owner. It's a must for teenagers to work there.

A few days before I was to start back to work, I was listening to the radio, and there was a contest to win a dozen doughnuts. WINNER! That was me. They wanted to know where I worked and would bring them there. Wow, that was a great way to start back.

I went into work for the first time in months, and the assistant manager snarled at me and wondered why I was back. Did I not win the lottery yet? So not quite a warm welcome back. I smiled, knowing doughnuts were to be delivered soon. The owner smiled at me and went to his office. I felt really good about this. Then the doughnuts arrived, and all the employees were staring at this delivery for me. I told the radio guy thank you and announced doughnuts for everyone. The doughnuts were from a big town capitol and a brand no one knew, and let me tell you, they were delicious. I was a hero. The owner came out of his office, and uh oh, we were all standing, eating doughnuts because of me. He asked the assistant manager what was going on. She pointed at me and said, "Ask her, your new employee." He asked me, and I told him I won them on a radio station and he should have one. He said no, but that was a hell of a good kind to win! He knew of this doughnut place because he goes to the big city all the time. I was a hero again.

So as work became more and more enjoyable, everyone's question was always "How long until she quits again?" I think they had a good money bet on it too. My boys were growing up, and everything was good. They were in school, and I had a great babysitter if there was a problem. She would always be there for me. I felt like I would be staying a while. I was learning more of my job. Unfortunately, I did not want to become a head cashier. They were always in trouble and would work more hours then I wanted to. They kept asking and asking me and soon quit, realizing it was not going to happen. I was treated a little differently because of this by the owner. I knew my raises would suffer from that too. I did not care.

The salesman who were coming in were quite entertaining too, always wanting a deal, never getting it because it would reverse, and the owner would end up getting it. He was so smart. Some of them came from all over: New York, Michigan, Ohio. A lot of them were Jewish, which made it more fun to watch them haggle over merchandise. I would always ask who was coming in today so I could work near the register to listen. As many as ten would come per day sometimes. Rarely, he would take them to lunch and always declined when asked to be taken. He did not want to owe them anything, I am sure. There was the hat man, the shoe man, the clothing men and ladies. Oh yes, how he enjoyed giving the ladies a time. They just were not sure if he liked them or not. There were also toy salesmen, camping salesmen, so many it is as if they were traveling down the highway and saw his store and would stop to sell him something. He usually did buy. They surely enjoyed him. If he was not liking the presentation, he would point at the oldest manager and say take over and go straight to his office. That meant goodbye. The manager would know not to buy anything.

The neighbors, Tom and Kiki, were quite funny too. They were up on the hill beside his house. Tom was a bit grumpy when he would come in to the store, always something wrong with what Kiki did or the owner did something to make him mad on the hill. Kiki was exquisite with her apparel. She was no bigger than a toothpick but always matched everything to the tee: dress, shoes, purse, and jewelry. She always chose bright, bright colors. She was nicer than Tom. I learned she was a dancer in her younger days and did shows. I don't know what kind, but evidently, she was a good one. The owner talked to her once in a while.

The customers were always something to talk about also. Some of them adored the owner and his store. Others came in, I think, just to give him a hard time. I never quite understood this. I always felt they should respect his earlier life and try to realize how it was in Germany. One particular couple, as in mother and son, would come in to shop and heckle.

I will get back to this periodically in my story.

Growing up, I liked to be a tomboy, which means I played all kinds of sports. My dad made me a nice basketball court behind the house near the alley. On the other side of the alley were some neighbors who had just moved in. They were German. They had a mentally challenged son. Unfortunately, her husband died shortly after moving in. So she started to talk to my dad on things to help her out around her house. She was quite cranky and strict. Her son was not allowed to talk to us. Dad helped all he could until one day my baseball went into her yard. She would not let me get it and would not throw it back to me. My parents were furious as well as me. Through the years, she tried and tried to make up for this. She brought my mom food. She tried to talk to her over the fence. She invited us to her house one day. My mom said we should go over and look at some history she wanted us to know. We went over there, and she showed us quilts, pictures, antiques of Germany. She was a nurse in WWII for Germany. Then as my eyes grew big, she showed us a picture of her giving Hitler flowers. I did not know the significance of this photo at the time. She said she had met her husband during the war and he was in the US Army. He brought her back with him, and they married. So Mom and she talked a little more after this day.

When I was working on merchandise one day, I looked up and noticed the owner talking loudly in an unpleasant voice to some customers, not that this was nothing more, only this time it was in German. Sure enough, it was my German neighbors who lived behind me growing up. I hid in the aisle because I surely did not want the owner to know that I knew them. After much bantering between them, they left.

This would not be the last of them in this story.

So as the days went by, I noticed I was always wondering where the owner was and what he was up to. Most of the employees would not want him around but not me. I was slowly learning about this man as a person rather than a boss. I was learning his moods and when to cut up with him and when not to.

Now everyone always said if you are getting further up in the ladder of this store, you will know it through him but maybe not through wages. One day I noticed on Mondays he always took the oldest manager to lunch, and you could tell that manager loved it. They always went to the same restaurant, which was very good, up the road. I started hoping someday that would be me without the manager part. Everyone is jealous of whoever got chosen. Well, after I got done writing up one Monday morning for the other store's merchandise to go down to them, I was walking up front, and he was out of his office. I always wore awful clothes on Mondays because I knew I would be outside in the lawn and garden, getting dirty writing up the merchandise. Sure enough, he said, "Susie"—wrong name, of course—"are you hungry?"

WHATTTT! I said, "Yes," and added, "but I have no other clothes. Thank you though," even though I was sad.

He said, "Get something off the floor that you like and put it on and come with me to eat and hurry up," or he was leaving.

I was so nervous and excited and then worried everyone would treat me bad from jealousy.

I picked out something simple and knew I had to hurry because there are two things you did not do when the owner says "let's go." One, never—and I mean never—ask "Where are we going?" Too bad, you lose. He will already be heading out the door. Second, never make him wait because, again, he would be out the door. So as I hastily went to the bathroom to change, I came back out and could not find him. I asked, to some unhappy people who did not get picked on this day, where he was. They just shrugged and pointed to the door. So I ran to his car and jumped in and said, "I am ready!"

The lunch was very good and classy. I felt like I was on top of the world. Conversation lagged some, but everyone there knew him, and it was just fun listening to them make over him. He made me eat a lot. He kept saying go back to the buffet again and again. He always asked if you were full. So when it was time to leave, he asked, "Do you want to take anything with you?"

I said, "No, thank you."

On the ride back, he drove very fast, and I had heard he got quite a few speeding tickets in his always beautiful cars he had. I now know that is why we were told to always treat the police and sheriff good. Give them what they want. We were almost back when he asked me if I had a good time. Stupid me said, "Yes, but it went too fast."

He chuckled with his belly laugh and said, "What did you want me to spend the whole damn day with you? It is time to go back to work, dingy!"

Yes, I felt stupid, and it was a long time before I got to go again. I got back to work and changed my clothes and went back to work.

I made such good friends working there also. One of my friends who worked housewares had a great garden one year and brought the owner in a bunch of radishes. He took them to her and said, "Thank you, but I cannot eat these. This is all I ate for many years when there was not any food."

We knew what he meant and never realized the Germans only gave them radishes to survive. She felt so bad but could do nothing about it.

My friend who would cashier with me was and is close to me. We had such good times harassing the customers but still getting our work done. We would go out at night too. During this time, we were gifted with some nice things. The owner gave us hams and turkeys. He started having breakfast on the day Christmas. Remember, it's also his birthday. We would get him a cake. He started giving us great bonuses at Christmas, along with candy, maybe a $100 savings bond once in a while too. He was trying to make us happy. He started a 401k plan, which to this day, I am so happy I have it. One year we wrote on the restaurant marquee Happy Birthday to him. We dressed up for Halloween, and one time I was a nerd looking like a man. He walked right by me and did not know it was me. They told him it was me, and he said, "Are you any smarter from this outfit?" He even enjoyed giving candy to kids.

One afternoon, a day before Christmas, my cashier friend and I said, "How about a birthday drink?"

He actually said, "Come in my office!"

We followed him, and sure enough, his holiday spirits were there. He poured us each a drink, and we toasted his birthday. We had about half a glass then went back out to run the registers. Sure enough, I did not know what kind of drink it was, but our faces were beat red from it. He came out and said, "What in the hell happened to you gals?" We tried not to show it, but we were very hot. He laughed and told the older manager he better keep an eye on us. Never did figure out what we had, but it was *gooood!*

During this time, he and his wife would travel a little more. She came into the store once in a while and was always greeted happily by us, or if he was out of his office, he would cut in and say, "What are you doing here?" She would reply, "Just wanted to say hi," and turn around and leave. We felt bad for her. We knew her job was to go around the other stores and compare prices for him. At night, she would repair returned items so they could resell them. She was quite a woman. They loved each other very much, but you always knew when they were having a spat. I heard she waited and waited for him to come home to eat, and when he finally did, she put it down the garbage disposer. He must have been really late. He walked, talked, ate, slept at his store.

I was starting to really enjoy new products we would get in. One item that comes to mind is the George W. Bush bubblegum cigars in a red, white, and blue cigar box. He was running for president, and somehow this was a promotion for him and the cigar bubblegum. It has a donkey on it also. So hidden deep in my closet twenty years later is this cigar box. I am sure it is worth a ton of money by now. So ha to all of you who made fun of me when I took it when it was empty.

Another time, it was after the holidays, the owner had them bring all the board games that did not sell up to the front to mark them down. One look at Candyland and I knew I wanted it. Not only did I love it as a kid, but my kids were going to love it too. So I asked how much it would be, and the owner looked at me and put a number 2 on it with a marker. I was so happy. What a deal! Yes, I still have this game with his number 2 on it. It's a keeper.

Our shoe sales were outstanding. One type of shoe catered to the little old ladies of the town. The Grasshoppers were famous at our store. The Saturday it started on was the busiest day of the week. You know how little old ladies can be. So we had to make sure they all matched when they came through our line. Heaven forbid, if they get home and the shoes don't match. It was a big day for the seniors.

One day I was driving to work from my mother's house when a man on a bicycle would not let me get by him. I was growing more and more angry by the minute. Finally, I sped by him, and he kind of went off the road into the grass. I continued on to work across the highway and was parking my car when the man on the bike found me and smashed his hand through my window. I called the police while he rode away. The police took the report. I called my husband and told him. My husband was coming into town that afternoon, and guess who he sees on the road on a bike? Yes, it is him. He stopped and asked if he just broke a window, and he said yes. He gave my husband his name, and he eventually paid for my window. During this time, the owner was concerned about my aggressiveness on the road. He told the story to his best friend, a doctor. This was the first, but not the last time, that I met him. Lots more on him later.

Anyway, the doctor came up to me and told me the world was crazy and that I should be aware of this. I said, "Thank you for your concern." Everyone wondered why this guy was such a good friend to the owner. He was Jewish, but things were just weird.

Things were still going good at work. I was learning more and more about the owner. His wife became ill one year, and he was devastated. She would need a huge surgery and would be in the hospital four to six months. We were all worried. We realized what she meant to him now. He would be up in the big city all day, every day. He hardly talked when he came in for mail. He did not care about phone calls or how the business was doing. He would stay for only a few minutes.

I learned he would show up at night and check in before going on home. So I kind of wanted to work nights so I could at least see how he was.

This is where "give a little bit" comes in. There is a song that goes, "See the man with the lonely eyes? Take his hand, you'll be surprised, and give a little bit."

PAM CROFT

One night, when I was working, sure enough, he stopped in, and one look at him told me how bad he was feeling. There was sadness in his eyes. So I just went right up to him and hugged him and told him I missed him. All the workers just stared with mouths open. No, he did not yell at me. He smiled and said, "Thank you." An explosion went off in my head. This man was human, not just a store owner, boss. He was a survivor, and he had a lot of feeling in his big heart. I think it was that moment that I was going to help him through this if I could. He had enough of bad life, and it was time for it to be good somehow.

My good friend who worked with me started hugging him as well. We were pretty sure he felt better on his nightly visit. We decided to put a note on his door to his office to tell him things would get better and we were looking forward to him returning to work and we missed him. He told the oldest manager that was nice but maybe we could paint his door since the tape made the paint come off and, please, no more notes. We looked at one another when the manager told us this with astonishment and ran to his office door for proof. Sure enough, there was a big piece of paint that had ripped off with the note. Whoops!

One Sunday he came in early and needed bills typed up because back then, that was how you paid your bills. I was cashiering that day, and the owner came out of his office and said, "Susie, can you type?"

I said, "That was the original thing I wanted to do in this job, but you never let me."

He said, "Come on." I was so nervous. He said, "Type this pile of bills up with these blank check." Wow, yeah, finally. I did it real fast, and he was impressed with my skill. I often watched him type, and he was a pecker. So after I got that done, I went back out and was a cashier again. Everyone looked at me like I was such a big suck-up. Oh well. I did not care. Feeling good about this, the owner came out laughing from his office with one of the envelopes I had typed up to mail. He said, "Do you not know how to spell Cincinnati?" I must have put three n's and three t's in it. How embarrassing, and I was brought back to earth, but I made him laugh when he hadn't in such a while. Over the years, he would always ask, "Hey, Susie, how do you spell . . . ?" And I would stop him and say, "Enough, please!"

I knew what hospital the owner's wife was staying. I got to thinking, what if my friend and I went to visit him? Would we be crossing the boundaries? It had been two months since her surgery. I asked my friend when we were working together. I said, "Do you want to go visit the owner up at the hospital with me and we can tell him everything is fine at the store, maybe get his mind off sitting there all day?"

She was hesitant but said, "Well, I guess it would be OK, but if we get fired, it is your fault."

I said, "Fine," and we set up a day to go, not telling anyone about this trip.

We drove up there all nervous and everything. We got there and asked what room she was in. We went up there, and there he was right by her side, reading something. She was not to awake and looked different from we remembered. We smiled and waved, and he said, "Come in, come in, please." He was very happy to see us. He tried to get his wife to talk to us and tell her who we were. After a few minutes, he went out in the hall with us and said we must be hungry. We got on the elevator and went to the cafeteria, and he bought us all kinds of food. He did not eat anything with us. We were still very nervous, and it was hard to eat. He stood up and said, "I have to get back up there." He thanked us and told us to be very careful going home. We said, "OK, take care, and we miss you." After he left us, we ate everything he bought us at the table, and we're so happy he enjoyed our visit. I told my friend, "I think your job is safe." Well, it was not only safe, but in our next checks, this man also gave us each an extra check for what we did for him! He said our thoughtfulness was amazing, and he was so pleased with our visit, so please accept this from him. WOW!

When I was working one night after this, someone said that the owner had to take his wife's car to the hospital that day because his would not start. Now his cars were always the best. That is one thing he did like to treat himself to, and he deserved it. He came into the store that night and pointed at me and said, "Susie, do you know how to drive?"

"Of course," I said. "Why?"

"Well, I came back and got my car started, so now I need you to drive my wife's car up to the house. It is sitting out in the parking lot."

I thought I was going to have a heart attack. Employees were looking at me like "there she is, sucking up again." I said yes and followed him to her car. He asked me if I knew where I was going. I looked funny at him because of the one night I bravely went up there. He said, "Of course, you know where you are going, you've been there before!" So I followed him up to the house and put it in the garage and did not even hit anything. Wow, he must really be trusting me now. So then he said hurriedly, "Come on, I am taking you back down in my car." So I jumped in his car, and he flew down the hill, as I remembered his driving skills, and said I was a big help to him. I said "thank you" and drove home feeling so proud and confident in myself.

So things were going great, and the owner's wife was going to get home finally. I remember when he started coming back to work, everyone was actually happy to have him back. I was relieved to know the store would continue on. No one was sure what he would do if he were to lose his wife. She was not in the best shape as before. She could no longer drive and had to have someone to be with her for the day. Eventually, the owner became his old self again and was pretty hard on us about the shape of the store since he had been gone. It hurt our feelings because we thought we did a great job. So as we were determined to stay busy at all times and continuously cleaned the store, a rumor went around that some people were making better money starting out than the ones who were there longer. Fighting was always happening, so guess what? I quit again!

Now this time I just left and went home and said, "I am done," again. My family looked at one another and said they were sorry to hear this but knew what could happen down the road.

After some months had passed, I began to get bored and missed my friends. I would call them just to get the scoop and to see if the owner was OK.

I went back in the store and said, "I am bored and think I want to come back."

The older manager said, "I don't know if this will work anymore. You can't keep doing this."

I said, "Come on, this will be the last time, I swear."

So he said OK and did not tell the owner I was coming back. I guess he thought that would be best.

My first day back was better yet. The owner saw me and just rolled his eyes. I think he told the manager that he was stupid for hiring me back. I was busy with something when the owner came out of his office and said, "Come with me." He took me over to housewares and asked if I knew how to run it. I said, "Sure I do," and he smiled and said, "Good," and walked away. "He's not mad at me," I told myself.

While I was gone the last time, a few changes had taken place. Where the grocery store was next door was now a military store. Beside it was a plus shop. Both were owned by the owner of our store. He was always thinking of new things to do, even though he was getting pretty old. He never stopped working. The plus shop was for heavy-set women who could not find clothes to fit them anywhere. The military store was surplus and new items, and that is how he first got started in business. It was like a full circle, with his department store, which there were three now, his plus shop, and now his military store. Wow.

It was easier now to work because my sons were old enough not to need a babysitter anymore. One day, while I was cashiering, the manager came up to me and asked if I would relieve lunch for the manager next door at the military store. I said sure.

Now this manager was in full control of a lot. He moved here from the South and somehow moved up the ladder quite quickly. The owner went on vacation a year earlier to Jerusalem, and while this man worked in hardware, he took him over to the building and said, "I will be back in three weeks, and you are to start this business up and running by the time I get back." Sure enough, he did a great job in starting a military store. It was soon booming—new life to our little plaza at the south end of town!

I went over that day and said, "Hi, I am to relieve you for lunch." This guy asked if I had ever come over to this store before. I said no but was willing to learn and I would be fine.

First of all, I have always loved the military. The smell was amazing in this store. I loved it. Later on, there were days that snooty women would turn around and go right back out the door because of the scent. Yes, this was going to be great. All those days of watching war movies with my dad is now going to pay off. Also, I knew the owner would walk over occasionally to check on things and make sure you were working, of course. I thought, maybe, this would be a great way to learn more about him since he was aging some.

So the second time I was asked to go over to the depot, I was almost certain it was time for the owner to come over, which was about a hundred-foot walk across, and check on me. He always walked over at least two times a day to see what was up. Remember, this was his new moneymaker for all the stores. I had a lot of customers come in each time, and I would enjoy learning what they needed because they would have to explain it to me since I did not know military names for items. I know I wanted to look sharp if the owner were to come over. Terms like "pick mattocks," "web belt," "P38," "entrenching tool," "gas mask bag," "pistol belt," and many more, I was learning each time.

That second time over—yes, the owner did come over—I remember glancing out the window constantly to see if he was on his way. Oh my god, here he comes! So I ran to the aisle and pretended I was straightening when the bells on the door rang open. I looked up and said, "Hey, how are you? I am just straightening the caps."

He said, "Are you supposed to be over here?" in a rough voice.

I said, "Why, yes, I have been doing this for a while now." I continued to blubber how I was learning everything about the store. He did not look confident in what I was saying. I said, "Rest assured everything is fine." Then I asked, "How is your day going?" trying to lighten the mood.

He said, "Fine, and make sure nothing gets stolen while I am here."

I said, "Of course, I will."

He went back over next door, and for sure, I thought, I would never get to come back over to GI store.

The next time I went to work, I looked at the schedule and noticed it said GI twice on it. I asked the manager if I was to go over to GI for lunches twice next week, and she said yes, that somehow he wanted me to go over there all the time for lunches from now on. She said it in a very jealous way. I was shocked. I asked why, and she said, "Obviously, he likes you." I really felt bad for the girl who had been relieving them for lunch and did not know what to say when, really, I was jumping inside knowing I wanted this more than ever.

Number 1: No more seeing the owner in bad moods all the time. He would stay next door with that bad mood.

Number 2: No more hearing all the bickering that goes on over there either.

Number 3: Getting to be by myself in my own store!

Number 4: The hours were different and better. Opening one hour earlier and closing one hour earlier than the big store. Yippee!

Yes, I was telling myself I had to get a full-time shift over in GI instead of the other store. I would succeed in this for sure.

When the owner would come over in a bad mood, I was determined to get him to smile before he would leave. That was my goal, not really to work but to learn more about him and see that he stays happy.

As I was working more and more at the military store, the owner also got us into a 401K plan. At first, everyone was leery. I jumped on board with it, and I am so glad I did. It turned out great. I wish I could thank him to this day about this. He also sent us birthday cards. He would sign them after picking one out of the card aisle then put a stamp on it and mail it to the store. We all thought this was weird but then realized he wanted you to know he did not just want to hand it to you. This was pretty amazing out of a millionaire. More and more, I was learning the person inside of this man who had been through so much in life. This man was good. A lot of people in town hated him, but they just did not understand.

As I was working at GI, the jealousy was felt from the big store. I didn't care.

I finally got asked if I wanted to work all the time at the military store instead of both stores. The manager at GI was becoming a good friend and insisted I come over for good. I said I was worried about the owner not liking it because it would be too much of me and it was a man's store. The manager said, "Nonsense, you are going to be here." I sneaked over to the big store and went to the owner's office and knocked. When I went in, I asked him what he wanted me to do. He asked if it was a good idea. I said I loved the GI and would be happy. He said I would be happy until I quit again! I said that was not going to ever happen again. He said OK.

So now we have three people at GI. One was a guy who was still going to college for business. He had been there about three or four years. We all started having a great friendship and fun when we worked together. We only could work together on weekends when it was busiest. The business was booming. A lot of times, we would have to call next door for help. The owner would get very upset if he walked over and we were busy without help. He would send someone over right of way. He did not like if we acted like we were having fun, of course. After he would go home for the night, he would often drive later on to check to see if I was OK and that everyone else had clocked out. If we saw him coming, one of us who was supposed to be out of there would run to the back and hide. He always wondered why our cars were still out there. We were just having fun even off the clock.

The guy who was going to college got his mom a job watching the missus up at the owner's house. She would always stop in before going home to tell us her events with the owner's wife that day. Some nights she would say, "Watch out, they are fighting." Other times she would laugh at the day trips they took that day. One time we all got in caught because the owner and his wife came down to the store and saw all of us standing around talking. He just stopped the car and stared in the door. We all knew we had to leave or get back to work whoever was working that night. It makes me smile and still nervous when I write about this.

My dentist was a Vietnam veteran and was a field dentist when he was over there. He was a bit of a puzzling man. Many never understood him either, but I liked him. When I was laid off way back when, he actually told me to come to his office. I went there, and he said, "Help me mold some dentures today, and if you like doing this, you have a job." So I did this for a day and did not like it at all. I felt bad and very gracious for what he did. He still loved military stuff. When we got in a bunch of dental surplus, I knew who I was going to tell about this. It was from Vietnam era too. He was so excited. The dental lights attracted him the most. We had about fifty of them. He bought all of them. Unfortunately, he came in to buy them when I wasn't there. The guy who was in college sold them to him at a discounted price. The owner got very upset. I just kept quiet. My dentist would come often, and I gave him deals as well. Not only did he appreciate it, but later on, he also helped my family with medicine that was needed for my dad and for me. He was a great guy. I do not feel guilty about the deals I gave him.

When people would come and buy, that you knew would take a lot of stuff, you often went ahead and gave the 10 percent discount. You just had to make sure you gave a good answer when the owner would come over asking because the owner would see them loading their cars. I think the owner had eyes in the back of his head.

I would run to the bathroom that we had knowing no one was in the store, and sure enough, the bells would ring, and it would be him looking like "how long have you been in there?"

One time an ex-bartender was hired, and I thought he was doing good. The owner came in and went straight to the register, pulled the tape, looked at the transactions, and pointed to no sales all the way down the tape. He looked at the ex-bartender and said, "You can leave now."

He never took anybody to court over stealing. He knew if something wasn't right. He would just tell shoplifters to leave. I, however, would get so mad I would chase them with a bat into the parking lot, very bad of me. I knew, when I had to pick the guy out of a lineup, that would be the last time I would chase anyone.

The customers were becoming regulars, and the stories I learned about the old store were good. I found out that the GI building used to have a bar in the back for Christmas, back when the owner ran it. He wanted his customer happy. That is why all the men received bottles for Christmas. Lucky men.

One day a gentleman asked me if we had cunt caps. I said, "Excuse me, but I don't know what you are wanting, and I don't appreciate your language."

He said, "Well, let me describe what I want, and I am sorry, but that is what we called them in the military."

Garrison cap, it is. So I asked the owner after he left if that was true, and he said, "Of course! What's the matter with you?"—this coming from a man who would tell you to smell something from a bottle and then squirt it in your nose. His sense of humor was so hard to outwit. Well, now I knew another work for a garrison cap and never had another problem when a customer would ask for a dirty hat.

I was starting to get closer and closer to my boss. Things were getting more relaxed, and I felt like I knew his moods better. When he would tell me what salesman were coming for the day, I would actually know them, the one from Michigan, New York, Cleveland. He would bring them over sometimes to the GI and ask if I needed anything from them. I, being totally nervous, would say, "No, thanks." I was learning how to check in orders and what price was paid for them. I was making signs after years of watching my manager do it. I thought, after four years of art in school, I can certainly do that. Everything seemed good. The manager of GI traveled some with the owner on business trips, all-inclusive with spouses also, everything paid for, and it would usually be to Las Vegas twice a year. Wow, what lucky people.

The manager would always come back and say how horrible it was. I would just say that I don't believe this and he was very lucky to get to go. He complained about everything. More jealousy from the big store over these trips. I just didn't understand. One time the owner's aunt died in New York, and the manager went with him to clean out her apartment. It was full of many, many things. He said it was awful, and I told him he should feel honored to have gotten to go. Eventually, the owner felt his ungraciousness and put him in a bad hotel in Las Vegas to try to straighten him up. It was already too late.

Friction was growing between them.

The one guy who was going to business school was about to graduate. The manager at GI was excited about this and told him he would have no trouble getting a big pay raise here and moving up the ladder. WRONG!

The manager of GI went over to the owner in his office and said that his coworker had now graduated business school, so let's give him a raise and a promotion. The owner said it would be a long time before that would happen and he should move on.

Now this coworker was the manager of GI's best friend, and this was a major blow to him. Things only got worse at this point.

The coworker, when told of this, became very angry and went over to the big store to talk to the owner. This did not help, and soon the coworker cussed at him and quit.

Now we needed to hire a third person, and the manager of GI was hot. He did less and less for the store. He would not show up as much. His pay was very high. He was salary. The people we hired did not work out for long. Yes, we were both missing the guy who quit, but we had to move past this. The manager just got worse. When the owner would ask me how the manager was, it was hard to say. I did not want to get in the middle of this. He asked me how many hours was he working. I would say I was not sure but he had to play organ at a wedding. This only worked for a while.

I still tried to keep upbeat and happy.

The manager of GI had started some really good outdoor military shows once a year. The newspaper would come, and military vehicles would line the parking lot for two days. We had so many people come and see. I enjoyed them as well as the owner. I thought this would help heal their feelings but was wrong again.

I was always scared that the manager was going to leave. Who would run this place? I never thought for an instance about myself.

The owner enjoyed coffee and tea. We had a small coffee pot in the back of the store at GI. What started as a treat for us turned into a treat for the owner as well. I loved making him coffee and hoped it would be just the way he liked it. Then when a really good coffee place came to town with tea, guess what? He liked the tea better. Every morning I worked, I made an effort to get him tea. They knew me at the coffee shop well. He appreciated it so much. He always tried to pay me for it. I said nonsense and would smile. Let me tell you, when Christmas bonus would come around, he gave me a humongous bonus. I did not like this and tried to give it back. Mistake. He got very mad, and so I said, "Thank you." I sent him a card as well.

His wife was still in and out of the hospital too. We just tried to make him happy when he would stop in. His health also was starting to show. He left for a few months, and I knew something was wrong. Finally, the manager of GI told me he was up in a hospital three hours away, recovering from kidney surgery. I felt helpless. I wished I could go see him. It made me realize how much he meant to me as a friend and a boss. When he came back, he looked older and tired. After a few weeks, he became a little stronger but never the same. So I thought now I need to help him if ever necessary. Going from hating this first job here to this.

The next time he was admitted was only one hour away for surgery. He told me this and said would be gone for one month. I asked where would he be, and he told me. Perfect, because my girlfriend worked as a nurse's assistant at the same hospital. I had info from day 1 on him.

I heard he was quite grumpy. One night we were visiting my parents, and I said, "I am going to see my boss now." They all looked at me crazy, and I grabbed my keys and left. I found the hospital, which was a surprise, and started to go to his room. Just then I saw the doctor who was his friend coming to visit him. I hid in a room. After a while, I asked the nurse if the owner's visitor was gone. She said yes. I went in his room, and it was obvious he was in a lot of pain. I said hi, and he was very worried his friend, the doctor, saw me come. I said he did not see me. He said, "Good. Now you can go." Yes, I was hurt.

I made it back to my parents', and they just looked at me and did not know what to say to what I had just done. Oh well, sometimes you just have to do things.

When he got back to work, he was different toward me.

He was truly becoming a friend, not so much as a boss. Here was a man who would bring us food from his home or a restaurant and made sure we ate it. On Sundays, it was French toast on Challah bread, then a few hours later, a trip to McDonald's to give us sandwiches. Here was a man who started bringing me souvenirs from trips he would take with his wife. This man did have a big heart.

After the owner and his wife got well, they decided to buy a condo in Florida for a winter retreat so they could enjoy the later years of their lives. He wasn't too keen on leaving the business but decided it was best for him. His wife really wanted to do this too. The first time, they left for about one week. I guess he called a lot over at the big store to check in. When they came back, they seemed happy. Then winter was coming, and he announced they would be going down to Florida for the winter. I was a little sad, while others were rejoicing. Well, after about two weeks, here they come driving up to the store unannounced. He flew out of his car going into the big store and just said, "What is everybody doing, just standing around? This is why we can't go to Florida for the winter. This store will never make without me. So I guess I will just have to sell my Florida home."

As it turned out, his wife did not enjoy being down there and asked him if they could just go home. "It was hot, and there was nothing to do. So let's just go home for good!" His mood was bad because now he had a full home of new furniture he had to bring up to his house by the store. He just couldn't win.

They still took trips, and on one of them, his wife had a stroke on the airplane. They made it back and went straight to the hospital in the big city. This was a long recovery period, but being the strong woman she was, she pulled through. She did not talk as well or move as good, but that was OK because he was still going to take her anywhere she wanted, even if he had to push her in the wheelchair himself.

You could start to see the wear and tear on the owner's face. It was hard for him to see her not as well as she was. One night, after I had just closed up GI and was walking down the sidewalk to my car, I felt a slow car behind me. Sure enough, it was the owner and his wife out for a drive. There were many times he would do this after I closed up, and he would roll down the window and ask the very important question of the night: Did you do any good today? I never knew how to answer this because I wasn't supposed to know the actual amount we did for the day. However, I taught myself how to read the tape at night when closing out the register. So I came back with the usual "We were steady today." Once I said, "You'll be happy." When I knew it was a slow day, I had to say a little slow because he would read it the next day.

On this particular night, he did not ask the question. He said, "Get in the back seat." I knew not to question or argue with him, and I nervously hopped in, knowing he was going to take off any minute. That is when the million-dollar question happened. "Did you do any good today?"

I squeaked out, "Yes, of course, it was busy."

His wife did not talk at all. This made me even more nervous. What was she thinking? Who is this idiot in the back seat?

He then said, "Do you want some ice cream?"

Finally, I knew where we were going. I said, "I sure do," with excitement because I love ice cream and they both laughed. Victory! I was sitting there with the boss and his wife and feeling just like part of the family. What will everyone say? They will be so jealous.

When we got to the ice cream shop, he pulled out a $20 bill and said, "Go in and get what you want and get my wife a vanilla shake."

I said, "What do you want?"

He said, "Nothing."

I felt bad about this. I went in and got an ice cream cone for me and her milkshake. I went back to the car, and he took me back to the store to drop me off. Nothing was spoken the whole ride back. I said, "Thank you and have a good evening."

When I got home, I told my family where I had been, and they just looked at me and said, "How nice."

This trip was not much, but it made me feel so good that he wanted me to go with them and even to help him out with the ice cream. I knew he was really starting to trust me as a worker and a friend. I wanted to help him more and more. I saw the change in him.

Now, during this time, my boys were getting older, and soon it would be time for my eldest to start driving and get a job. Where do all teenage kids get there first jobs? McDonald's, of course, but when you live in my town, our store also. So I asked my son if he would like to work at the big store, in hardware. He did not seem too excited about this. I told him he would not see me because I would be at GI. He said maybe. I asked the owner if this could happen, and he said he did not care. My son worked in hardware for about four years. Even on summer college breaks, he would go back. I loved it. I did not get to see him much, but I sure liked when I did.

One thing we had in the summers at GI was a huge military show right there in the parking lot. People would bring their military vehicles and Humvees and National Guard soldiers. It was amazing, excitement everywhere. The newspaper would come and take pictures. I felt great being a part of this. I was loving the military more and more. I would dress up in camo shorts and a Marine T-shirt. I thought I was big. Business would be booming.

This was the year videotaping was becoming popular as long as you had a video camcorder, yes, the big one. I think it was around 1997 that my husband bought one for us, and I knew I was going to take it to work on the owner's birthday, for sure. I learned how to use it and took it in on his birthday. I was going to have one for him and one for me. It was a surprise, and I thought he would enjoy watching it later on to see his store and employees honoring him on his birthday. WRONG!

I waited forever for him to come over so I could use it as soon as he came in the door. The owner always was taking pictures and carried his camera in his car. When he came in the door, he immediately put his arm up in front of his face and said no. I turned the camera off and said OK, knowing my next move would be next door at the big store when they brought out his cake.

So as I waited patiently, the phone call came and said, "We are ready to give him his cake." I anxiously went over and started recording the employees and the store. Then the moment came, and the owner, my boss, came out of his office. We all sang "Happy Birthday" as I was recording. It went very well. Then I noticed one of the longtime employees who was assistant manager of the big store was not there. I asked where was she, and they said, in the bathroom, crying. I went down to the bathroom with my camera ready to film her, and sure enough, there she was, crying in the bathroom. I asked what in the world was wrong, and she said the owner had just told her that he loved her after thirty years of service. I was so happy to get this on film. She just didn't know how to react since he was such a hard man to figure out.

From there, I went into his office to film one more time before his patience would run out on me. I remember laughing as I went in, and he glanced at me from his desk and said very low toned, "Are you about done with this?"

I said, "Yes, sir, and I will be sure to give you a copy of this." Then I left. So he has a copy, and so do I.

Current update, my son had just purchased an old VCR machine and had said we should watch it, but I have not gotten the courage to do so yet.

As business was booming, the tension between the owner and the manager of GI was growing. The manager was talking of leaving more and more. I think most of it was salary and not being there the number of hours to which the salary was paid. I was getting more nervous as I went into work. There was no way I was taking the manager's side on this issue. He was making very good pay to my little pay. He was getting trips and not I. Things were now very bad between them. The manager of GI would say to me, "I hope you are ready to run this place." Panic was inside of me, but I knew I would do it if needed.

One day the owner came over and asked to have a hammer. We thought this was odd, but we did give him one, of course. He went down to the end of the building with it. After about a half an hour, he came back looking tired and puzzled. He mumbled to us, "I put something in the concrete block when I helped build this, and now I cannot find which block it is." All just stared at one another. Is it money? We were wondering. Is it jewelry? Is it papers? To this day, I don't think it has been found, and I only hope if they ever tear the building down, I could be there to witness what this is. We all still would love to know and think about it.

So when the time came for the manager to find another job, he just said goodbye and never got offered anything by the owner. When the manager would visit after this, once the owner spit on the ground at him. That is how bad it became.

Everyone was wondering who would run the GI store now. I took it upon myself to start making signs, doing the schedules, ordering, and so on. Still, the big question was who. I assumed the owner was now going to be it as he was over at GI a lot with me, and we really clicked on what new items to get in and just how much to try at a time.

After a few months, he was in there with me, and a customer had question. He said, "You will have to ask the manager," and he looked right at me. I said I think you should ask the owner, and I looked at him. This is how I became manager. One word of advice from him was always keep your nose clean. I have never forgotten this.

I started offering my views on new things to have in the store. Women's clothing was one of them. It was hard to convince him of this as he wanted it to be a military-slash-hunting store. When I showed him women's hunting apparel, he just said, "I don't know about this." Finally, I asked the salesman on the phone one day to call him and tell him how important this is. He agreed to this, and sure enough, the owner came in and said, "Go ahead and try a few items of women's clothing." Guess what? It sold like crazy! Finally, I was getting the retail world.

I continued with the military shows in the parking lot. This time I knew of new people who had a great big collection. They would spend the night in the parking lot. My son came over and helped me with this show. It was so much fun. The owner was amazed at this. The Army Reserve came with a Hummer. No one had ever seen one up close before.

Paracord bracelets were becoming the new survival thing. As we all know, paracord had always been a needed item for the military, coming off the parachute that you would jump out of then cutting the cords so it could be used in survival ways. Many a day I rolled paracord into rolls to sell after cutting them off of parachutes. What a seller. Now it was made in many colors, bright, camo, red, white, and blue. You name it, we got it. We had a supplier close by who made the best rope, and they became our way of making a lot of money from this. I told the owner, the more, the better. It was a very hot item. People came from far from hearing of our selection and great price. Oh yes, I was becoming a success.

Now let's go and remember family and customers in this book.

Family would come and visit often. They really weren't supposed to, but now that they knew I was over in the GI, they knew they could come and visit. I was always nervous when they would show up, constantly looking out the window for the owner. If he would come in during a visit, I would introduce him. He was always short and nice then would leave as I wondered if I was in trouble from this visit.

Mom and Dad, he liked my dad, not so much my mother.

Brother and sister-in-law, kind of could not believe how big my brother was.

Aunt and uncle, tolerated them visiting as my aunt would try to make over him.

Sister Ann and Aunt Beatrice, yes, I said Sister Ann. This was really nerve-racking. Remember, the owner is Jewish. He embraces my aunt, and she kisses him on the cheek, and he was thrilled. He did not understand Sister Ann, so I had to tell him how my family was somewhat split in religion because my grandpa wanted one daughter not Catholic. Yep, that would be my mom. I still believe we have Jewish in us from facial features plus our last name. My brother and I found a jewelry store in Cleveland with our last name, and we went there, and they were all wearing caps on their heads. "Oh yeah, we are Jewish," I said. Also, the owner came in one day and told me their new rabbi had my maiden last name. So I said, "Told you so," smiling. He loved to call me by my maiden name in an abrupt voice to see me jump. Every time, I would.

When we went to Cleveland once to a deli, sure enough, some of the customers looked like my relatives. I just don't know.

He always asked about my aunt Beatrice from that day on. She was pretty, and he liked her.

My dad thought it would be a good idea to bring my uncle in from St. Louis, even though I was meeting up with them after work. When they came, it was in the afternoon. We were busy, and they had a few drinks in them. They were happy. I was not. My dad decided to grab a military sword to look at it and, of course, swing it around. He swung a little too much and literally knocked the tip of it off. He looked shocked and wondered what type of merchandise we were selling that would break so easy. I said, "Thanks for breaking it."

He laughed and said, "I can fix this. Don't tell the owner, and I will weld it back together."

I agreed to this, and they left.

A few days later, Dad brought it back welded together quite nicely. You could see a little line in it, but I was sure it would still sell.

Of course, the owner came in and looked around some days. Sure enough, he looked at the sword one day. He said, "What happened to this sword? Did it ship here like this?" I could not ever lie to him, though I wish I could have, so I told him what had happened and assured him I would sell it. He growled and said, "Bring your dad back in and see what else he can break."

That hurt a little bit, but I understand his anger. Near Christmas, that sword did sell. I even showed the customer the line, and he was fine with it. I couldn't wait to tell the owner. When he came over, I told him the sword had sold, and he said good. Wow, out of trouble again.

So things were going great. My family was growing up. My job was the best it had ever been. Business was booming. New ideas were being accepted by my boss, so I really felt the business side coming out of me at this time. I knew I was not only a friend but a business worker as well. I felt as though the store was my responsibility, and I was going to take it as far as I could. I am sure my friends thought I acted different during this time, but business is business.

I suggested a really good military show to bring in to the parking lot. They had a ton of everything imaginable as far as vehicles were concerned. They were good customers as well. They brought at least seven different types of vehicles. They would spend the night in the lot always mentioning the next day how busy the lot is in the middle of the night! My son participated with me in this weekend event. It was nice, although his excitement was not as big as mine. My boss took pictures of it all. That is how I know he approved. This show lasted for about three years every summer, one weekend in July. People came from all over to see it and stopped in from the highway as they went by and saw it. A helicopter even was brought in one year.

Then there was the year when people were getting worried about the world situation, and prepping would be the smartest thing to do. Everyone was scared, and just by luck, the big city news people called me and wanted to come film to educate people on surviving. WOW!

I went and told the owner about this newscast that would be happening. I told him he needed to be in it because he started this business in 1950 and he knew everything. He said, "No, no, no, you will do fine in the taping." I pleaded with him, to please at least come down from his home to watch it because they were filming that evening. He again said, "No, thank you."

The news people showed up and wanted to have gas masks on display, along with other surviving items. So we brought out the MREs, light sticks, first-aid, water tablets, etc.

We all were so nervous. Real news people you see on TV were right in our store! Just as they were trying to guide us as to what we were going to do, I glanced out the door, and I saw the owner driving by slowly. I shouted out, "There is the owner, let me see if I can get him to come in." Well, it did not take much coaxing.

He slowly got out of the car in his oh-so-cool way and said, "What's up?"

I said, "You know what is going on, and you need to come talk to them."

He shrugged and went into the store. They all rushed up to him and started asking him all kinds of questions. He saw the camera and became more shy than I had ever seen him. He fumbled nervously, and I now knew why he did not want to come see this. He was not a bragger on anything. He finished the interview, and I managed to get my hands on camera holding a gas mask for the camera. It was a good day.

I now knew he was not a starstruck person. All the times he went to Vegas and saw all the show up close, treated greatly, he did not care. He said Dean Martin had the biggest feet he had ever seen. He said Jerry Lewis had the biggest mouth and put a glass in it. He said Don Rickles made a comment about his wife during a show, and they hated him from there on out. He loved Jack Benny. When I think about it, they were similar in their actions.

We had a lot of customers who were entertaining as well. A woman whom we called Tina Turner would come in very high strung and funny and nice. She would wear a mini dress and would always buy things for her dad. She was a hairdresser. The owner got cornered by her one day, and he looked like he did not know what hit him. One time the actor from *Police Academy* came in because he was from our town. I was staring, and the manager told me he is shy so don't make a big deal out of it. He only talked a little bit and then left. He passed away not too long after that, and I wish I could have told him how funny he was in those movies.

Now I will go back in the story about my German neighbor who lived behind me growing up. For some reason, she kept coming into GI and would try to talk to me about politics, my boss, family, etc. I hated this. My boss would see them come in and would get furious. I think she did it to get at him because she would always say, "I did not kill his family, Hitler did."

She kept getting rewards for her amazing life and being such a great Republican in the city. She made front-page news twice. I knew this hurt the owner every time. It would say what a great nurse she was for the US Army during the war. There I was reading this, knowing she was a nurse for Germany. So I asked the owner, "Do you want me to take care of this?" His eyes looked up from the paper, looked sad, so I already knew the answer.

I got on the phone to the newspaper and told them they needed to stop putting her in the paper or, better yet, research her for her nursing in Germany and giving Hitler flowers. I told them I was a neighbor of hers and saw these pictures growing up. They were astonished at this. They apologized and said they would look into this. Never again did she appear in the paper, and I am still happy I did this. The owner thanked me.

My mom was a great seamstress. She was so talented in many ways, but her personality was sometimes hard to understand. She was very set and stubborn in her ways. The owner and she had their share of fights.

So the years kept flying by, and before long, I realized I had been back for ten years! Somehow I knew this was where I was going to stay for good. I thought. Anyway, that is later. I was eventually hiring my own people with approval from the owner. Some good, some bad, as always. I made really good friends who are still my good friends today. One of them I still visit and talk to every week. The only problem with this person is that he was a senior in high school with ambition galore. He was model material and wanted to go to Hollywood after he graduated to pursue his acting career. He also made short films.

He came in and needed a lot of props for his latest project. I told him we did not loan out merchandise for this, so he suggested he would work here and borrow it while he was an employee. I thought long and hard on this, knowing the owner would not agree to this. So I just decided I would do it anyway without letting the owner know. He was very entertaining, and every girl who came in fell in love immediately. He said he was leaving in three months to go out west in a van.

When the owner met him, right away, I felt tension. There was no immediate click at all. This was OK because Barron only wanted to work Fridays and Saturdays. The owner was not around much at this time because of Shabbot. They rarely saw each other.

Well, my friend did as he said and was gone in three months. He kept in contact all the time. He came back every so often, getting more and more jobs and being recognized in Hollywood. The employees next door also liked him and were very excited for him.

One time he came back after five years, and the owner came into the store, and Barron was standing right there by the front of the store. I very nervously said to the owner, "Remember Barron? He used to work here."

The owner somewhat glared at him and very quietly said, "Vaguely."

That was about it, and the owner turned around and left. I was embarrassed, but Barron just laughed, and so we still talk about this today. More on Barron in my next book.

My second son was ready to go out and start his employment ways. He received his driver's license and knew it was time for a job. So he decided to follow his brother's ways and join the big store across me. His eldest brother was already through college and on his way to his career.

I asked if my youngest son could work here, and of course, they were pleased. I was nervous, of course, because whenever you have a family member working for you, you only hope things go well. They did, of course. The owner actually liked both boys. This one, he talked to more. This one was going into banking, and so the owner loved this.

My mother kept visiting me at the GI. She was a bit bored. The owner asked her if she knew how to sew. That was a silly question, seeing how she made all my outfits growing up. She said, "Yes," and he said, "You're hired!"

Oh nooooooo! Now I have two family members here working.

I asked him point blank, "Are you sure you want to do this?"

He said, "Of course, I have a ton of surplus material and an industrial sewing machine that needs to be used."

My mom asked, "What would you like for me to make?"

He said, "Bags, lots and lots of bags. Then you can come up with items as well.

I now realize how good this store was to me and my family in my life. If the owner liked you, he would do anything for you and your family. He might be grumpy about it, but he would do this for you. I wondered if it was the European way. I think he just did have a caring heart for family since he had lost his. Anyway, I am very grateful for this and wish he knew this.

As time went by, too fast, my son went on to college and did become a banker. He interviewed for the biggest bank in town, the one the owner was a member. He got the job. I am not so sure the owner did this for him too. He asked me if I wanted him to say something to the president about my son. I said, "No, thank you." My son got the job right after the owner went to the bank. To this day, I still do not know but have a hunch something was said, and this only proves what kind of a man he was.

As life was going by too fast, I started to realize this is my destination, the store and helping the owner any way I could as he aged. Our time together, I felt, was becoming more and more valuable. His relatives were starting to visit more.

My business mind was doing really well. I could not believe how things were clicking with the business and knowing all along what a great teacher I had.

As the seasons passed by so very quickly, one memory that sticks in my mind is the dreaded jeep of 1960-something. That was the way we would clear the parking lot. It was a tiny thing, and the steering wheel was on the opposite side. It did not have a muffler or heater, and I often wondered if it came from the war. So many charley horse would happen as the men would try to maneuver it. I was dying to take a ride in it, and one day I got my wish. Of course, the boss was not around, so I ran out of GI and flagged down the unlucky driver. It was freezing that day, and he stopped and asked, "What is wrong?" I told him to let me in because I wanted to see how bad this jeep really was. Well, yes, it was really bad. There was only half a floor in it! Fred Flintstone would know how to drive it, for sure. I was shocked at how cold, loud, and terrible it was. I never questioned the men when they would come in to get warm any longer about wanting sympathy for the jeep. They got sympathy from me that day on. Many people wanted to buy this jeep, but the owner never did sell it.

It never failed that while my mom was working there, she would manage to take a smoke break when the owner was visiting me at GI. A lot of employees smoked. The owner was not as nice to some as he was to others, and my mom was the one he was not nice to. The tension was growing between them, even though she made great items on the sewing machine. I was mixed between emotions on having her there. When she would finish her cigarette, she always peeked her head in to say hi. This routine was getting old with the owner. I understand that smoke breaks were to be short, and as for the ones who did not smoke, they never got a break. The owner was a retired smoker himself, I learned. He could light two ciggies at once and smoke them from each side of his mouth during a meeting with salesmen. A heart attack in Las Vegas when he was in his forties cured that addiction.

So my mother eventually left for another part-time job. It was sad but a relief at the same time.

The salesmen were coming every week. Traveling salesmen were becoming a thing of the past because of online ordering, but the owner would not have this. He did not own a computer at this time. The manager was starting to do some of the meetings as the owner was getting older. One thing the manager said was if the owner gave him a look and squeezed his hand like a ball was in it, that was a sign. The sign was to squeeze the balls tighter until the salesman gave him the right price. When the owner stopped squeezing his hand, you were good to go with the deal. Very interesting.

Phone orders were still the way to go for ordering also.

To this day, I do the same type of ordering rather than online. You get better deals when you are sweet talking a real person rather than a machine. I would love going into his office with a list of items that we needed, and he would say stay here and listen. He would call the company up, and it was so amazing to hear him dicker and dicker with the cleverest lines and win everything he was going after. My, this also taught me well.

My part-time job had been turning into full-time in a flash. I was doing displays, creating ads for the paper, schedules, ordering, and many more things for the GI. I loved it. The owner and I would fight but, after a few days, would be fine. You always knew when the fight was over when he would bring you food, and what good food it would be.

My father was starting to age as with the owner. The owner had some work done about two hours away and then a gallbladder removal. This always would wake me up as to how fortunate I am to see him. My father, however, was diagnosed with cancer.

The owner was so successful. His business ways and charm were a perfect match. "Keep your nose clean and you'll do well" was one motto. When women would come through the door, he immediately would say, "Hello there, ma'am. My, you're looking well today," then of course, "Is there anything I can help you with?" The ladies would gush and walk on. When the men would come through, he would say, "Hey there, old buddy, watch you need today?" One time a man was looking at some leather jackets, and the owner jumped on this opportunity. He walked out to the isle and said, "Oh yes, what a good deal we have on these leather jackets." The man just stared at him and went on looking. I was ready to take bets on this sale as I was convinced this would never work and he was only looking stupid to the customer. Well, shows you what I know. The owner then said, "Come on, try it on," as he took it off the hanger. "Come on, it will look great on you." He held it open so the customer would feel like he should slide into it. The customer actually did just this. "Now look in this mirror," the owner said. Sure enough, the customer walked to the mirror. "Yes, it is you. It looks so good on you. Only $60 and you can wear it home." By now, I was hiding behind the counter, embarrassed all to hell. I was laughing with it also, and the owner knew I was watching the whole time. Guess what? I rang that jacket up, and the guy wore it home! "And that is how you do it," the owner said to me. Did you learn anything? Yep, paint a pretty picture, and they will buy it. To this day, when I see a victim walking to my merchandise, I try the same routine, and most of the time it works.

Even though the owner and my mother did not get along, he still admired her sewing abilities and how she could be a great seamstress. He always asked, "What happened to you? You're not like your mother at all." I, however, was very good at the art and loved making the store new signs weekly. Unfortunately for me, he was good at art too. He would always present me one at least once a month, which I must say looked amazing. I gave him my high school canvas paper notebook and asked him to please draw me something in it. Well, about four months before he passed away, he gave me it back and did not draw me one thing. I was so mad.

So as we started to get closer and older, my dad came in the store when he was very sick. He sat in a chair up front just wanting to see me. The owner came in and saw him sitting there. Up until this point, the owner knew Dad was sick, but just then he realized how sick he was. He was a bit nervous all at once looking at my dad and asked, "How is it going?"

Dad shrugged and said, "Your guess is as good as mine."

The owner said, "Good luck, old buddy," and promptly walked out.

After that day, the owner would always ask what I did on my day off, which he knew, and how is my dad doing. I also think he remembered how my grandpa, my dad's father, would stop in and buy gloves in the tent during the winters. My grandpa worked the highway, which was right next to the tent.

The tent was a very important, signature in this story. It was how he started and how he got the land the big stores were on now. It had to have been so cold in it during the winter, but I am sure the stove was warm for everyone when lit. I think the owner must have slept in it also. I wish I could have seen it. When someone mentions a tent store in my city, we all know whose it was.

After Dad passed, I worked more and more. The owner was somewhat my second dad now, and it felt good. I did start giving him

Father's Day presents. I know, right? What do you get a very rich man who is your boss? I always thought they were stupid gifts. Of course, the ties were very hard. Standing at the store for an hour just staring at the right one in a lower priced department store than he would have gone to. He often said, "Let me pick my ties. Not you." He always liked food. So some Jewish treats were a good idea if I could find them. I never thought he cared a bit about these presents until one time, when his health was very bad, we got into a huge fight, one of many. Father's Day was around the corner, and I made up my mind, no more of this. A week went by, and we started talking again, and sure enough, he said, "Where is my Father's Day gift?" I about threw up. I said I forgot and was very sorry. Now I know how he felt about these stupid little presents. He loved them. I wish I would have given him one that year because it was the last time I could have.

The surplus was booming at this time still. The sales were online or by phone calls. The owner would go up to the big city and view the items up for bid. The manager before me went with the owner all the time. I could only wish I could go and root through the great military items up for bid. Dreams do come true. One day a big sale was coming up, and the owner walked over to the store and asked me if I was ready to go sniffing through surplus. I about threw up again. I said, "YES! When?"

He said, "Tomorrow morning."

I said, "YES!" I did not care if anything was going on. I was going there.

We met up the road a way because the owner had other business afterward and did not want to drive all the way back. First of all, we ate lunch. That was a surprise. We went to a Greek restaurant close by. The owner, a Greek man, knew my boss quite well. The food was terrific. I complimented the Greek's jeans he had on. They were very classy, very expensive. I told my boss how they must have cost a fortune. Sure enough, a few months later, my boss was ready for his first pair of expensive blue jeans. He had them tailored to fit him perfectly and did not care about the price. He asked if I thought he was too old for them, and I said no way. He said they were heavy to wear. He sure got complimented everywhere he went when he wore them. Even at the store, the customers would say, "Nice pants!"

Now back to the surplus. We found this huge building, one of many, and I felt like I was in the military finally. This base was amazing. Soldiers everywhere. When we got to our building, we were greeted with a man the owner knew well. He gave us a paper, and away we went. The owner knew all the aisles. He told me they always put really good items at the top of the box, so I needed to dig through the tri-wall to find other gold inside. I know this does not sound like fun, but to me, this was heaven. I waited so long to do this. I rooted like no other rooter ever. Yes, I got dirty, but I did not care. I would actually yell out good items that I had found. I felt like I did a good job because this was one of many trips we did to get our surplus.

I only hoped there would be no jealousy with my new buddy, the owner. Other workers saw what was happening. I did not care.

We started going more places. The owner was getting older, and driving was more difficult. He always said I would know all his little secret places for shopping. He was ready to give up one of his three stores, the one furthest away. The town was medium-sized. His store had done well over a span of thirty years. What does he do? He doesn't sell it to make money like everyone would think. He donates it to the high school for their wrestling team matches. Yes, he was so kind to do this. Do you think they were appreciative of this? At first, they were. Then three years later, the school sold it to a hardware company and made a bunch of money from this. The owner was not only hurt by this but angry as well. I felt bad for him.

I always knew when he was upset at something. His mouth would give it away with the way he would hold it.

My work friend of many years was ready to go see her daughter over in Germany. Her daughter's husband was in the military, and they lived over there. She wanted to know if I would like to go. I did want to go to see where my husband had been when he was in the army and also to see where the owner had been during the Holocaust. The trip was a lot longer than I had expected. Boy, did I get homesick. It was a great trip, however. My friend's daughter was so good to me. She was a great tour guide as well. The Germans were not the friendliest. When we were dining, it was the anniversary of WWII, and in the streets, white supremists came barreling by us yelling. I was very nervous. We just waited in the restaurant until they were gone. That was my first big feeling of only what the owner went through during the war. *This is crazy,* I thought. *How can they still be like this after all these years?* I bought a phone card so I could call home. I sure used it too. I called my husband, then my mother, then the owner. I tried not to cry but told them all I wanted to come home. My husband said, "It would get better." My mom said, "Settle down." The owner said, "Go and have a good time and see the good things over there." On our tour, we went to Salzburg and spent the night. I called my husband to see if he had been there before. He said no. I called the owner and asked if he knew of this place. He said, "Of course. Is that where you are? I spent many a night there after the war."

I felt such happiness because he sounded happy about this. I slept a lot better that night. On the last leg of our tour, we went to a Holocaust camp. This was when it hit hard what the Jewish people went through. I could not put into words this place. Yes, it was one of the camps my boss was in. After this, I was so ready to go home. I knew I would never want to come back to Germany. I was flying back alone, and the airport said they did not have a seat for me. I about had a heart attack. They made me stand against a wall with other people. None of us understood this because we all had a seat on our ticket to fly home. They said they were overbooked and we might spend the night. My friend had already left to go back to her daughter's house. I was in such a panic. English was not great, and the signs did not make any sense. They pointed to a hotel across the street if I did not make the flight. I waited an hour, and finally, there were two of us left, and they called my name. I just know, when we landed in the blessed USA, I cried in the bathroom for a good five minutes.

Upon my return, I felt so differently about the owner. I knew we were getting pretty close, but now the situation changed. I was glad he was not unhappy about me going over there to Germany.

He started saying things about takeovers of the business after he was gone. I just said I could not continue there if he was not there. He said retirement was in his future. He arranged a meeting at a local hotel in the restaurant area. It was to be in the evening, and all department heads were to be there. He had the accountant as well. I was feeling really sad. There was five of us there. We talked for about an hour about his retirement and how we could take over the business for him and actually own it by paying him an incredible low loan. It was a great deal. We were to think about this and discuss it to see if we could all get along with this process. There would be other meetings in the future with the decisions. Everyone was excited except me. I did not want this to happen. They all knew this.

So after this meeting, nothing was said, and no one tried to organize this takeover, which made the owner very disappointed. The manager of the big store who was there, at this point, thirty-something years did not even want to talk about it.

As time passed, the owner have certain procedures done with his health. The next one I believe was the exploratory one, which he felt something was wrong in him. He had already had kidney cancer, and they removed half of his one kidney. He managed to convince us he was on a trip when this happened. We believed him. When the exploratory surgery happened, it took a toll on him. Relatives came and helped take care of his recovery. I did not see him for some time. I knew I was going to keep the store in great shape so that when he came back, he would be proud. Sure enough, he was very pleased with the store.

His driving was getting more difficult to do. His eyes were growing old also. Our sales were still doing great. The owner's wife was also failing in health. She now needed people to watch her all day, and then he would take care of her at night. He would make sure she would go out to eat every night if possible, no matter how hard it was to move her. He would be very worn out every morning when he came to work. If his office door was shut, that meant leave him alone; he was trying to rest.

One of our surplus shows was approaching out in Vegas. It was a big show and needed to get great deals and seasonal stuff. I was always hoping to go. He had gone by himself for a while. He would always suggest how I should go to. I would always get my hopes up, but then it would not happen. There were two shows a year. I would have to make up the list of what we needed, then write the companies that had the best deals. He started taking the manager at the big store with him. I was angry at this. He would take his wife and the manager's wife and a caretaker. One time he went on vacation before the show and, when he came back, called the big store to get the list off me and bring it to his house to take to Vegas the next day. He did not even call my store. Was I mad? Hell yes! I had also bought some nice clothes just in case I was asked to go. When the owner got back from the show, I expressed my anger, along with throwing something, and he shrugged and said maybe next time. We did not talk for a week.

People would know when we were fighting. He would avoid coming into the store, and I would not bring him tea in the morning. He would stay over at the big store all day. He would look over at my store but turn around and walk away. When he felt as bad as he could, he would finally come in with some food to make up. Guess what? It always worked. Then things were fine again for a while.

The time finally came for me to shine with a trip to Vegas. I finally was asked one day, "So do you think you would like to go to Vegas?"

I hesitated for fear of being tricked again and calmly said, "Yes, I am," when really I wanted to scream, "Of course, I am, you damn fool! I've only been waiting for years!" So he told me when to be ready for the flight, and there would be four more going: his wife, the caretaker, the manager next door, and his wife. I thought, *Well, what about my husband?* but did not say anything. I thought it was not fair. I still asked my husband anyway, even though he would have to pay when the others did not.

He said, "No, thank you." He encouraged me to go and have a good time and shine.

I was so nervous. One thing on getting to go was a rule: Do not let the other employees know you are going. I thought, *Now how is this going to work?* These people were my friends and were suspecting this all along.

Sure enough, the woman I had grown to love and went to Germany with asked me, "Are you going to Vegas this time?"

"No, of course not," I said.

After the trip, she befriended me for lying to her. I could not help this.

So I was ready to go shine and went to the airport to fly out with the other manager and his wife who did not like me either. The owner went on another flight with the caretaker and would meet us out there. I was asked by the owner if we could all get along on this trip. I guess he was worried about friction of some sort. The owner would be staying in another hotel across the street from us. I would be cuddling up with the caretaker. How about that? I did not care. I just wanted to go. We would meet for dinner the first day out there. I was ready for a drink. I thought I could chug a few before dinner and not be found out. When we went to the hotel where the owner was staying, he told us to wait outside and they would be down. I saw another opportunity to chug again when I turned around and there, lo and behold, was the owner staring at me. I threw that drink in the trash and tried to be normal. Everyone loved my situation, but I never knew if he knew I was drunk. All he said after dinner was go to bed, be ready to work tomorrow morning after breakfast, and do not go out gambling. "Yes, sir," we said.

The caretaker came to the room after she made sure his wife was in bed. She talked and talked, on and on. Finally, she's asleep.

The next morning, we went to the owner's hotel for breakfast. He was there all ready for the day. The manager of the big store came in looking quite a bit tired. Then I realized he had gone out for fun. He gave me a look like "shut up." The owner was telling about his younger days in Vegas and how he was well-known, how he was respected out here. He had seen a lot of famous people: Dean, Jerry, Frank, Don Rickles. He was keeping my attention when all of a sudden, the manager made an "ouch" sound. I looked at him, and he had just broken off his tooth from a bagel. He again gave me a look like "don't say a word." I tried not to laugh but did not succeed. That bagel left a huge hole, and I don't know if he ever got it fixed, but I sure talked about forever.

We had to hurry through the meal to get to work. When we got there at the convention center, it was just like surplus heaven. I got to meet all my clients I talked to on the phone. I got my own name badge. I was in charge of getting my papers out and getting the best deals, shaking hands and being introduced as the owner's right-hand man for the military store. I was shining just like I wanted. Never will I forget this feeling. The manager from the big store already knew his hardware people, so he would go off and do his work. It was good seeing faces with these voices over the phone. Even where we got our camo shopping bags were there. I was worried about overspending. So many orders to fill.

After a brief lunch, back to work again. Two floors of companies, I was getting tired. Finally, time to go back to our rooms. But remember, we were meeting for dinner. So little time to get ready but I made it. We went to a beautiful restaurant, treated like gold. The caretaker and I had to take a separate vehicle. After dinner, we were told to get a ride home. The owner would pay for it. We waited for a taxi when a nice shining black limo pulled up. We waited until the people got out of it and asked if we could sit in it. We were allowed and took pictures on our phones of each of us in there.

The next day we met for breakfast, and sure enough, the owner asked what time did we get in. I said we went straight back but got a great ride. I showed him the picture of us and the limo, and his face dropped and became angry. I laughed and said, "Relax, we took a taxi, and we just sat in the limo, that was all." His mood was a non-believing mood the rest of the day. After we worked and was on our way back to the hotel, it was decided that there would be no dinner on our last night there. Whatever we did was up to us. So I just did a little gambling, shopping, and eating and went to bed. The owner was flying out the next morning, and we were to fly out that afternoon. The caretaker and I decided to sleep in and go swimming over at the owner's hotel until our flight since the owner and his wife had already left. I was a little sad that we did not get to fly back with them. The pool was great, and the weather beautiful. When we got ready to fly home, we went to the airport and met up with the manager of the big store and his wife. Boy, he sure looked hungover and funny.

I asked, "What is wrong with you?"

He smiled and answered, "Just still drunk that's all." I laughed, and he said, "But boy, are you in trouble. Both of you."

The caretaker and I looked at each other and said, "What are you talking about?"

He said, "We tried to call you this morning to find out why you're not at breakfast."

I said, "No one told me about breakfast."

He said, "Anytime you travel with the owner, you are to have breakfast with him."

I fought back in panic and said I was not invited. He said the owner just figured we were out late and drunk. I said, "No way." So I instantly tried to call the owner before our flight to tell him the misunderstanding, but there was no answer. This was the longest flight home since Germany. I was so worried I would lose my job over a breakfast.

When we got home, I decided to just not call him anymore and wait to see him the next day.

The next day came, and when I went to thank him for a wonderful trip, sure enough, he asked, "Where were you for breakfast?"

I explained that I did not understand the rules and was sorry for missing it, but we enjoyed the pool that morning instead, and had he looked out the window, he could have seen us in our bikinis. He asked if my phone was on, and I said, "No, so I did not know you called, but thank you for letting us use the pool." After that, he was fine.

Sometimes I would get in trouble for not sharing my merchandise with the other stores. I felt that if I did this, no one would visit my store. The owner always said to share, and I would disagree. Sure, I made people mad, but I did not care. One of the people who would order me flags and hats took it out on me when

I needed more merchandise. He would say he would order, but three weeks later, he still did not. I finally decided to find my own merchandise and get it. This guy would be a major problem in the future. I think there was jealousy involved also.

Now this story gets a little sadder. My mom had been sick for quite a while ever since my dad had died. We managed to take trips together, but more and more, it was getting harder for her to breathe. I thought her grieving period never went away. She would say how badly she was missing my dad and her mother, that she did not feel good and could I do more things for her. Of course, I did this but still encouraged her to get out more. She had asthma and was a smoker. You know where this is going. She eventually was diagnosed with COPD. She was very stubborn and counted on me for everything. She was now on oxygen and was very moody. She quit wanting to go gambling, which was one of her favorite things to do. I tried to get hard with her instead of babying her. Her sisters did not know how to help her as they did not live near her. My duties were increasing daily. My husband and I wanted to take a little overnight trip, but my mom was cranky about it. We fought a lot that day. She wanted a sandwich brought to her when I got off work before me and my husband's trip. I was not happy about this. She wanted me to sit down and talk with her. I told her I had to go. She just looked at me and said, "Do as you wish." She said she did not feel well. I told her to call my brother or go to the hospital if needed, that I would be back the next day.

The next day, when I got back, I went to get my check from work. I went in to say hi to the owner, and out of the blue, which he never says, was "How is your mother?"

I said, "Making me angry."

He said, "Go and check on her, and quit being like that."

I thought this was weird of him, but I did what he said.

I went to the house, and the door was locked. I used my key to get in. There was my mom lying on the floor at the kitchen. She would do this when she could not breathe. It would help her. I said, "Mom, wake up," and she did not move. I said, "Mom," and went to move her, and she was cold. I immediately called 911 and went outside in shock. This was the worst day of my life ever. The police came and did their job. I still did not understand why no one called me before this. She had a rough night and talked to her sister and neighbor, but they did not know this was going to happen. She told them she did not feel well and her breathing was bad. I saw where she never ate the sandwich I brought her the day before. I wish I would have stayed for sure that day.

My mood was horrible for months. I was drinking badly. I was trying to deal with this while cleaning out her house, the house I grew up in. I was trying to work and still be a good wife. My aunt and uncle helped clean the house out. I never hurt so bad in my life.

My mom had been gone for one month when the owner decided to have another meeting about his retirement and the takeover. His wife was becoming more ill at this time. I was never told about this meeting. The manager next door at the big store asked me if I was going. I was shocked. I said I did not know of it and asked when it is. He said in two days. So the next two days, when the owner would come over, I never asked and just waited for him to tell me. He never did. I went and got drunk the night before it because I was off the next day and was not going to the meeting. I was very hurt again.

The next day I was recovering from my hangover, feeling sorry for myself, when the phone rang at the exact time when the meeting was to start. It was the manager asking me where I was. I said I was not invited, and he said the owner thought he told you. I did not believe this.

I said, "I have not showered and have a hangover, so forget it."

The manager said, "Get your butt in here, pronto."

So there I was walking in, no shower, hungover, and late. The meeting went bad as no one was getting along. The owner wanted to know what we decided. All five of us had not even talked about this takeover since the first meeting. We just stared at him, and he was very mad. Not much else happened of these meetings after this, and I blame all of us for this because we were all scared of hurting his feelings when we were not sure he was ready to give the business up.

Two months after my mother's death, I was at work, and the owner came over to see me. He first asked if I was drinking last night. I said no. This would always make me mad, but really, he did know when I did. He had a magazine with him and opened it. There were teen models in it wearing polo shirts. Spring was approaching, and he asked me if I thought these shirts would sell. I said my son would wear them. He got so angry and told me he did not care about my son and this had nothing to do with his question. I was hurt again and furious. I said, "I was just letting you know these shirts could sell with that age and older." He left mad, and I knew I would not be coming back. First of all, no one came to the memorial for my mom from work. Second, you do not mess with my family.

So I quit again and for good, so I thought.

This time I had been back for nearly fifteen years or more. It went by so fast, a long run for me. Why ever go back? I always asked myself this. He does not care, so why should I? I always remembered he lost his family in a horrific way. I now have lost mine in a more normal way. I felt bad for him always. His father was a hosiery and sock salesman in Germany. I had seen the family photo on his wall at his house, and he sure looks like his father. This picture always stuck with me as well. I knew why he was like this. At least five camps took years of his life and took his family. He was so lucky to have survived.

So now what? He was not getting any younger. The 80s was upon him. His wife was not getting any better. She was not good at all.

The next five years were when we bonded the most. But unfortunately, we fought the most too. I think the daughter thing was there. I was glad of this. People knew this too.

I decided to take care of my mother's estate with my brother before ever dealing with the owner again. I needed to grieve on my own. I knew this would take quite a while, but I did not care. I felt like I cared too much about work at the time she died and should have been there more for her. I was angry at the whole situation.

About a month into working at the house, my coworker called me and wanted to know how I was doing.

I said OK but still had some things to do with the estate. He then told me the owner wanted him to call me and to tell me to give him a call. I exploded and said the owner could call me if he wished, but I would not call him, although I missed him and my job. My coworker said the owner asked every day if he knew of any new news on the girl, who, of course, was me after all these years. My coworker said the owner was miserable and told him he did not know what he did to upset me so much. Wow, this was typical of him to say this.

So another week went by, and my coworker called again, saying the same thing. "Fine," I said, "I will call him when I am ready." I waited another week and called him. He was at the doctors and asked me to call back in a little while.

I waited a few hours and called back, hesitant as to what to say. Of course, he started off with "When are you coming back?"

I said, "That is where you just don't understand. First of all, no one came to the memorial from the store. Second, you don't give a damn about my family. Third, you don't realize all that was put on me, and I still have a lot to do."

He said, "Meet me at the grocery store tomorrow so we can talk more." I agreed to this.

Trying to stay tough as nails with him, we met. I got in his car and said, "Now what?"

He said, "Are you coming back?"

I said if I even did come back, it would be another month. I needed time heal and finish up. He said he never meant to hurt me with his comment, but it was a business question that needed answered with a business answer, not with family. I did not know whether to be madder at this or let it go.

I let it go. So I said, "Maybe in a month, I will return."

He said, "Good, now let's go grocery shopping because I need to get food for the house."

I knew my job was already back with this venture because it would soon be happening all the time.

So I waited for about a month as I wrapped up the duties of the estate and went back.

I was now going to be his driver when needed, run the store and other things. I was somewhat excited about this. The owner was now entering his mid-eighties, which I could not accept because he still acted sixty-like when I met him. His wife was slowly going downhill, and his health was also starting to show signs. I knew it was now or never to spend more time with him. I was treated great. The store was doing well.

One time the meeting was still trying to happen. He really wanted us to take the stores over for him. Unfortunately, we were too chicken to do this. We were afraid of hurting his feelings and letting him down. I had heard he was having one, but he never said anything to me about it. I felt like he just did not want me there. He had it at a local hotel meeting room. I was hurt he did not say anything to me, so the night before, I, of course, drank myself happy. I was off the next day when the meeting was taking place. I was still grieving over my mom. So I had a hangover, and the phone rings. It was the big store manager, asking me where I was at. I said I was not invited. He said, "The owner wants you here now," and just assumed I knew. I went to the meeting looking very rough. Oh well, nothing ever came out of these meetings, which is very sad.

I started knowing his doctors well and his extended family that was all that was left from the Holocaust. Cousins were mainly it with nieces. I am not sure what they thought of me.

I started to take him to his doctor's appointments. He loved his doctor. His eyes were going bad with macular, so he needed injections in his eyes. That was not fun, and he was very mad about this. His heart was doing weird things. It was missing beats. We went to a faraway hospital to see if he could be a candidate for open-heart surgery. I was against this, but he was not. Thankfully, the doctor told him he was not a candidate for this. Was I ever relieved.

We once were supposed to fly to Miami to an eye doctor for his macular. He would do anything to save his eyes. We made it to Atlanta and then had to turn back because of weather. I was also relieved of this. He let it go from there on.

We were together every day, except my day off. I just went with the flow knowing it was not going to last forever.

He needed to go to the big city every week, and I learned it so well, all the roads. Fridays were the funniest because we would do the Jewish thing for Friday night. We would go to the Jewish store to get challah bread. We would go to the grocer to get Jewish candy and pickles and canned goods. He always would ask what I wanted, so I eventually knew what item I was going to get that week. From there, we would go and eat lunch at one of the best places in the big city. There were about five choices, so we rotated them, and it was great. Sometimes we would go and get merchandise for the stores. He always knew when something was available at a good price.

One day he said get in the car we are going to the big city. I never asked. I would just grab my coat, purse, and yelled for coverage for the store. As we were driving, he motioned me which exits to take, and we ended up at the car dealer.

I said, "You don't need an oil change yet."

He said, "I know."

I just figured he needed to ask them something. His cars were always the best. That was one thing he pleasured himself with—a great car: Lincolns, Cadillacs, now Lexus.

While I was sitting there at the car place, a man came out and said, "Almost ready, sir," to my boss.

He said, "Let's get out and wait."

I asked, "For what?"

He said, "You will see."

Sure enough, a new Lexus came around the corner and stopped. The man got out and said, "Here you go."

My boss thanked the man and looked at me and asked, "Are you ready to drive this?"

I was stunned and said, "No way." Even though I know he should not be driving, I said, "You are driving this first. This is your car, and you deserve it." It was beautiful.

He tried to fight this, but I won. I knew I was going to be very nervous, but I told him I would guide him to get to the bakery for bagels. This was the longest ride of my life. I think he went through two red lights and out of his lane maybe three times, but with my help, we made it. I took pictures of him in this car and love these pictures to this day. After the bakery, I drove the new car. It was so fun and exciting and nerve-racking. When we went home and pulled up to the store, I had no idea what the people thought that I worked with, but I did not care. I wondered if they thought it was my new car.

So all things were going well, except for the owner and his wife getting older.

I knew so much about him, his moods for sure, and there was plenty of that. His facial expressions said it all.

A slow wink as you walked by to clock was good. It meant "glad you are here," and the store will be fine. A quick exit to his office meant we were either fighting or he was going to leave. A grandma shrug after a one-liner meant he was happy and thought it was nice what was just said. He would crinkle his nose at the same time as the shrug and smile. Grasping his pants and pulling them up strongly during a salesman visit meant he did not like his offer and would get him to come down on price somehow. And he always did! Buzzing his office for a phone call was a real treat. He would pick up with that voice saying yes, and I would panic and completely forget who was on the phone for him. I would just say "shit," and he would yell, "Write it down!" His belly laugh was the best. If anyone could get him to do this, it meant victory. Chomping his teeth meant thinking about turning the sales pitch completely around to benefit him. Tongue out while writing meant he was doing something artistic or trying to screw something into something. All of these were great quirks of him.

So as I went back again, somehow I knew this would be the final time to do this. He actually needed me. People saw this, questioned each day, like "Are you driving him today?" "What is on the schedule for you two? So we know when we can relax."

When I returned, one of all the first things to do was take him to a cemetery for a burial of a friend. Wow! I felt very mad at this but told myself I returned to this and it was my fault. I don't think he even knew how it made me feel. We did not talk about Mom much because he claimed not liking her. My friends at work would always remember her as the lady who would dig under the pop machines outside for any change she could come up with. She would often come into the store and ask for a yardstick because she saw some good change under them. I tried to tell her it was not her money, but she would say finder's keeper. She did well with this sometimes.

So as my life was changing, which I knew it would, the owner's wife was getting worse and worse. He tried not to accept this. I am sure he had seen enough death in life and did not want to see this. So we kept on working and driving.

One day we were scheduled to go North to a mop and broom factory. It was a big place, and we had gone once before. On our way there, I thought the owner acted a little funny. After we made our purchases and was heading back home, his phone rang. It was the nurse who was watching his wife.

She said, "Where are you? You need to come home. She is not doing well, and time is ticking."

He said, "We are getting close," and said goodbye. We were still an hour away, and I saw fright in his face. He asked if I wanted to get lunch. I felt bad for him. He did not want to see any more death. I said, "No. I think we should get home."

We got back, and I let him out and got my car and went home. They said he went up to the house and brought his niece down to the store, even though they said it was not a good idea. His wife passed away, and they called him to come home. He was so devastated and not good.

I did not know how to approach him after this. It was a day, and then the funeral would take place, being Jewish. I still did not talk to him. My coworkers and I went to the funeral. He had his nurses helping him and staying with him. He was not functioning well. I told him how sorry I was at the funeral, and that was it. I still did not know what to do. After a few weeks, he tried to come to work with his wife's nurse helping him. I thought at the time, *Is he going to die too?*

We would talk briefly because he always had someone with him. His relatives started coming around too. Now they knew their chances of getting all his money were really good. He kept me at a distance, which I was not used to.

He kept getting sicker and sicker to when he did not want to get out of bed. I finally got a hold on myself and said it was time to make a stand about how I care about this man. None of his relatives knew I had been driving him or anything. They were all shocked at first when I went up to the house to help. They looked at me with nontrusting eyes. The man who was supposed to be in charge of his will was there from another state. He was very mean to me. He kept asking me questions, like how do I know the owner. I was pouring the owner a Coke, and that man came up and smelled the Coke and said, "What did you do to this Coke? This does not smell right." He poured it out and got another one and said, "I will give the owner the Coke, and you can go." I knew at this moment how bad and crazy these people would be.

The owner had a lot of helpers, young ones as well. They could not be trusted either. This was when I knew taking care of him and running the store was going to wear me way down also. My family would suffer as well, but I did not leave. One worker he liked and the other worker had been with him a long time. He was getting grumpy with me and said I was not the best caretaker. I was hurt again. One night one of the nurses called and told me the night nurse had a lot of visitors in the driveway and that she never drove herself. I thought this was weird but did nothing at the time.

I had gone to a ballgame and drank a lot. I got home that night, and the phone rang, and it was the nurse. She wanted me to know that the owner was talking and eating again. I asked if I could talk to him. I was so excited. It had been two months long of sickness. We talked, and sure enough, I wanted to see him, so I got in my car and left to see him, much to the disproval of my husband. On the way there, I managed to hit two deer, but I made it, and the owner was already back to sleep. I woke him, and he got mad and told me to leave. I was so hurt. He said, "You are drunk, go home." So I did.

The nurse that night just looked at me and shrugged when I left, which made me furious. When I went back to work, the other nurse told me that the night nurse did not have a driver's license. What? Lo and behold, there, they came the next day, and she was driving the Lexus and him. I marched over to his office and looked at them and said, "I believe you do not have a driver's permit."

The owner looked at her and asked, "Is this true?" She denied it. I said, "Then let's see your license, please."

She said, "I don't have it."

The owner said to her, "You can leave now and don't come back!"

I felt bad but knew this could get him in trouble and the drugs being delivered at night would stop. I slowly resumed my driving again.

My husband and I went on a much deserved vacation to Washington DC. The owner was still sick but getting a little better. We took Amtrak to Washington, which was very nice. They told us at the station to park across the street because a world summit would be going on when we got back and the city might be shutdown. We did not worry and went on our way. We got to Washington, and it was great. I went to the Holocaust Museum, of course, and found his name on the survivor wall. I took a picture of it when a worker asked me if I had a connection. I said yes. He told me if I had information, he could find many more things on this person. We ended up finding letters and all kinds of information on the owner. I was ecstatic. He copied everything for me to take back.

When we got back, I made the owner a book of his past letters and things. I was so excited to do this.

I arrived at the owner's house a day after we got back from our trip. He was eating breakfast when I came in. He always was in a good mood at the table when he was eating. His eggs had to be just right to be the happiest. I learned how to cook them in this unique way and still use this method today. He asked how my trip went, and I said good and that I had something for him. He shrugged in his usual way that meant he was a little jealous of me leaving. So I told him about the museum and was very nervous about this. He said some of his friends had visited the museum also. I pulled out the book I had made him and explained the whole story, and his eyes started tearing up as he took the book. I had to help him read the old letters he had received because his eyes were not as good. The problem was it was in German. So he got his magnifying glass and desperately tried to read each one, crying along the way. He was so thankful to me. This was probably the most heartfelt thing I had done for him. He did not know whatever happened to these letters. Now he knew how important he was to me. His relatives had tried to reach him while he was in the camps. Some made it, some did not. He showed this book to his relatives when they would visit. Wow!

So now he was getting back to normal but still needed nurses to help at home. I became the day driver while still trying to run the store. My husband and my sons were doing well. My sons had good jobs. My eldest was working for a newspaper out of state. My youngest was getting ready to graduate college and was busy with his band writing songs and being the lead singer. The owner always asked how they were doing since both had worked for him.

My mother always wanted her ashes to be scattered in Las Vegas after she passed. We agreed that I would do that for her. Well, the time had come to do this. My eldest son wanted to go along with me, and I thought that was great. We planned a nice trip with some extra things to do, one of which was to get on a game show. More about this soon.

<<Where this page starts at So now things were getting back to normal it should be on page 41 along with the rest of this story here.>>

I told the owner that I had to go to Las Vegas, and he asked when. It just so happened there was a buying show the same time we had made our flight reserved, which I was not aware of. He told me, "I am going out there the same time by myself for the show for two days, if my wife is well enough for me to leave." Panic went through me. I was in no mood to work on this trip that was already sad enough for me.

I said OK, and he said, "No, wait, how about you meet up with me and go to the show?"

Screwed! I said I could try but was not sure. One thing was sure, I was going to be working out in Las Vegas. I told my son I might have to work a little bit, and he was fine with this.

Off we go to Las Vegas with my momma in the suitcase. We got to our hotel, and I was already getting phone calls from the owner as to whereabouts. It was a very early flight, so it was early out in Las Vegas. I told my boss I would be down to the show in about an hour. Then I told my son I would be back in a few hours and we could go party. He said fine.

I grabbed a taxi to the show, and there he was, waiting and ready to work. After two hours of working, my phone rang, and it was my son, asking, "When will you be off work?" I said soon. He said he was already two sheets to the wind and was bored. He wanted to come to the show. I explained to him that he did not have a badge and I would be there soon. I told him when I get back to the room, we would go to dinner and have fun. He said OK. I was getting a little anxious. After flying to Vegas, I was straight to work, and now my son was drunk all before one in the afternoon!

It was nice seeing all my phone buddies for ordering merchandise. I felt like a bigwig, right-hand man, indeed. He was finally going to ride a scooter instead of walking. I know this hurt his pride but was proud of him. He knew all the people, of course, old and young. They respected him as he strolled by them, always calling to him. When I would place an order, he would move on, and I had to find him.

The owner and I finished up at work, and he asked me what I was doing for dinner as he needed to eat. HELP! I told him I needed to go to my room down the road and could come back at seven. I suggested he take a nap or go gamble. I grabbed a taxi and went back to my room. I was ready to eat with my son. Unfortunately, he was passed out on the bed. Now what? Well, I got ready for dinner with the owner and grabbed a taxi and went back to his hotel. I asked him if he could eat now. He said his legs were hurting badly for some reason and he could not go but asked if I could go get him something to eat. I said sure. Meanwhile, my son woke up and wanted to know where I was at. I told him and said, "I will be back soon, and we could go eat."

I was really starting to get hungry myself at this point, but I found food for the owner and took it to him. So far, I have spent more money on taxis and food than gambling and fun. The owner asked where my food was. I told him I would eat with my son. He said, "Go have fun, and be there in the morning for one more day of work."

WHAT? "OK, sure," I said.

Waking up starving, I knew I would have breakfast at the show.

So I grabbed a taxi again and headed back to my hotel. Feeling like I was in a movie, I got to the room only to find my son passed out again. So I got into my pj's and crashed till the morning. I woke up and told my son that I have to work one more day and then we could have fun. He was not happy at this point. I could not blame him. I got ready for work and grabbed a taxi again. When I got down to the owner's hotel, he was ready and feeling better. Then his phone rang, and it was his nurse, saying that his wife was not feeling good and needed to maybe go to the hospital. At this point, I could not lie. I kind of breathed a sigh of relief. He loved his wife so much. I knew what he would do. He hung up and said, "Help me pack. I have to go home now."

Still no food for me!

Within an hour, he was grabbing a taxi and heading to the airport, saying he was sorry. I waved goodbye and grabbed a taxi and went to my hotel and celebrated time with my son. We went to the park where my mom wanted to be spread and scattered her. Then we went to eat and gamble; we ate first.

The game show was later that day, and yes, my son got up on stage for name-that-tune. All the people were older than him. Next thing I knew, my son crushed it and won every time. He ended up winning $200. He was so happy. The host, who was the host of newlyweds, asked him how he knew the songs so well. He said in his part-time bartending days, people always played these songs.

I got called up on stage for card sharks game and lost in the first round. Oh well.

A snowstorm was on its way to the Midwest, and guess what? We had to fly home early also. Maybe my mother was getting back at me for something? You think?

So back to page 43 after the book giving.

Driving him became fun. One problem was my youngest son writing music. I always had a new CD of it. Yeah, I made him listen to it. He never would say anything about it, but his face said, how dare me when he likes classical. I think it was nice of him to let me do this. After all, we fought before about my son. The fact that he did help him get his great job at the bank makes me think he was just as proud of my boys also.

Well, let's move on with the driving part.

He wanted to go to more places since he was feeling better. This led to me driving him more. That was OK with me because I knew it was what he needed to stay alive after his wife passing. His way of alerting me of a driving day was not good. It was more like him saying as he came to the store, "Are you ready?" I would just say yes, growling to myself.

It usually happened before my day off so he could keep me longer, I think.

We would go two hours for ice cream.

We would go shopping and was a struggle for him. His phone would keep acting up, so let's go an hour away to fix it.

We would go to old friends' places in towns about an hour away just to say Hi.

The best one I remember was the day he said, "Let's go," and I got ready, never asking where. When he says "let's go" that way, I say OK feeling a little burned out from this. I knew we were heading a ways away from our town but still drove silent.

When we were two hours away, I asked, "So where are we headed?" thinking to myself I should call my husband to let him know if I would be late.

He said, "Just a little longer. There is a great grocery store that the warehouse man said was over this way, with all countries of food in it."

I said, "Where would this be?"

He said, "I think another hour away, but I am not sure!"

So I got my cell phone out and asked it where this Jungle Jyms is. I followed directions and still could not find it with my patience almost gone. I pulled over and asked a man about this. He said, "Just down the road." We finally got there, and it was amazing—all kinds of food. The owner was amazed as well. He found an item that his dad used in Germany when he was a little boy. He bought this and gave me some of it. Not realizing the time and remembering how long it would take us to get back, I called my husband, and he was tickled about this trip while I was not.

When we got back to town, it was late. The next day I asked the warehouse man, "Hey, heard you've been to a great store with food." He said yes, and he told the owner about it. I said, "Maybe you should take him sometime since you like it." He said maybe, knowing he did not care to do this. I said, "Wait a minute, you don't have to because I had to, thanks to him." He tried not to laugh, and I said, "I will get you back for this." Later on, I did with the driving.

So as time passed onward, so did we. One thing he wanted to do after his wife's death was get well enough to take me on some trips all related to his past. The first one was to St. Martin. Wow, I was never so worried in my life. What if he gets sick and dies? He was not worried about this at all. He wanted to show me where he and his wife loved to go. So guess what? We went. I had to be the driver, of course, along with the navigator and also be a nurse to his medicines. The first place did not suit him at all to stay there. So we moved on. The second place was very pretty and nice. Unfortunately, after a few days, I woke up in my bed and was covered with bed bug bites—very bad reaction. So I called for a new room, and they came up with a cleaning team to fumigate our room. I said, "No way, we want a new room." After going down to the desk and threatening to reveal my body for proof, they agreed to a new room. They accused us of bringing them in our luggage. The next problem was our car. I had to go get it one day to drive us, and coming around a corner, I thought I was in our parking garage. Well, it was a garage but only for people, but I kept driving through this garage, and it got smaller and smaller until my car was stuck against concrete walls. I must have been tired or something and realized what I had done. So I slowly backed up with very bad scraping noises, and now knew I had damaged the car on both sides.

But you know what, they charged him for repair to that car months later and never ever made me pay. Oh sure, he showed me the invoice but then just shook his head.

The next trip would be to San Diego, which was good because I have a cousin who was living there at the time and I had not seen her for years. It was a good trip, and of course, we fought a bit, but all in all, it was fun. My cousin came to see me. His cousins came to see him.

His cousin Pauly—I am not sure which side of his family he came from—was nice to me.

So after these trips, which I am grateful for, for I got to see parts of the world that were great, we went back to work. I, of course, was a caretaker and manager of a surplus store.

I was really starting to become more Jewish at this point. I started driving him to the synagogue on Saturdays. On the first try of this, I dropped him off and went shopping while he did this service. All his friends were there, including the doctor that is very bad. They all looked at me strange when I dropped him off.

So it was getting close to picking him up. I pulled in, and he came out talking with the doctor. He got in, and we went to leave, turning down the road when he said, "Go the other way so we can eat." I got all frustrated like normal and did a U-turn right then and there. As I was coming back up the road, a police car put siren and lights on, and guess where I had to pull over? You got it right, across the street from the Synagogue, where all his friends were standing outside talking but now looking at us with the police car. Great first impression, right? I tried to get out of it best I could, but sure enough, he smiled and gave me the ticket. Unfortunately, it was filed under his car since I was driving it.

He was not happy at all. I told him it was his fault for making me turn around. I did pay for that one, however, and from then on, he got the warehouse man to take him to the synagogue.

Other things were happening too. He fell in love with all the children's Jewish songs. So since I was not in control of the radio, I learned many Jewish songs. The dreidel song is my favorite.

I was still driving him when I asked him one day if he would like to go to a bar for a drink. I needed it bad. To my surprise, he said, "Yes, I would." So I took him to a place that was pretty big, and sure enough, he got up on a stool and drank a beer with me. This is a great memory for me. It was the middle of the afternoon, and the people just smiled at us, wondering what the heck we were drinking for.

He knew I was drinking more and more because of stress. He actually knew when I had a few the night before. In the mornings, first thing he would say was "Come over here so I can look at you." Yep, every time he would know. I guess even with macular disease, he still could tell.

Speaking of which, his eyes were really bad by now and made him more depressed. We tried all kinds of doctors, and they would inject the same way, but nothing was working. It was sad.

We are at a point when this story becomes very hard to write, so I would like to give a glimpse of how the owner lived, even though he had all the money in the world.

His cars were about the most glamorous things he owned. They were either Lincolns or Lexuses. He loved his cars.

First of all, his outstanding clothes were actually very old. They were top notch and looked amazingly new all the time. He never liked to dress looking like a bum. When I started going up to the house more, I noticed more and more things. This little house, which was quite comforting, was dated around 1960. The Brady bunch had nothing on him. Before, this house was a log cabin someone had built a long time ago. He and his wife moved into it and then built the house. The new house was very cool. The front room had huge windows overlooking the city. It had a piano in it. He never told me it was for his wife, even though he knew how to play it. You see, he had lost his index finger over in Germany during the Holocaust. I heard two things: One was he was working in the camp and hurt it cutting down a tree. The second thing was a Nazi had chopped it off. Still, I do not know which one is correct, but I do know the way it was stitched back together looked very bad. So this is why he would not play the piano anymore.

The wall in the front room had a family portrait. It did not matter how many times I had seen this picture, I still would want to see it when I would enter that room. The family he once had whom the Germans took away just made me realize once again what this man had gone through in life, how he never saw them again that last day. Oh yes, relatives told his father to get out, but his father had faith and said it would never get that bad.

The picture had his mother and father in the front row; his father looking just like the owner was looking now, his mother gentle with a small smile on her face. The owner and his two brothers were behind them. They were all very handsome. The owner, being the eldest, was behind his mother. The middle child was next. Then the youngest brother was behind his father. The funny thing was he was looking not at the camera but at the owner with a smile like something had just made him laugh. He had very deep dimples. I asked the owner what made his youngest brother laugh and look at him. He said he did something funny to him but would not tell me. It sure made the picture more precious.

As you walked through the middle room, there was a bookcase dividing the rooms. It was full, of course. Then there was a credenza with Jewish items on it. One day I noticed a paper taped to it, saying, "Dr. Credenza." That was when it hit me. This doctor was already grabbing what he wanted when the owner would go on to his next life. This was very upsetting to me.

As you walked on, back there was a bathroom, then a bedroom to the left and a bedroom to the right. The bedroom to the left also had a back bathroom. The kitchen was to the left of the middle room. The middle room was so big, it had a dining room table.

Now the kitchen was amazing as well. It had a toaster that made the bread rise on its own. Never had I seen such a thing. The cupboards were full of very old fine china. There were two silverware drawers. That is what the Jewish people do, and I never could figure out which one to use. He would let me know as soon as I brought his food in.

The left bedroom had a mint green bathroom, which was beautiful, along with a phone. Yes, that was his bathroom. I think the right bedroom was his wife's later on because he never could clean her items out of it when she passed away.

His heat and water were all in the attic. This was odd and bad whenever he had a problem.

So as I learned the house, the cooking came next, and I am so glad it did because I now know tricks to good cooking. I know Jewish preparation when cooking is taken very seriously. I first tried broiling some steaks in his oven, which was above the stove. I did not know a fire could start if you had the broiler on too high. This sure did happen, but I managed to stop it so fast that he never knew. He just thought I might have burned the steak.

The true honor was when Passover was soon to be, and he asked me and a caretaker if we could cook it. We said, "Yes, no problem," and was so excited to do this. He sent us to the store for the supplies, which were hard to find since our town was not so much Jewish-savvy.

Well, this meal took us forever to make. He was getting anxious because I think it had to be done by sundown. He actually helped prepare the table setting, and it was beautiful. Now I saw what a lot of these items were actually for. The meal was good but not great, but I felt such a closeness to him and now knew more of the Jewish traditions.

The driveway to the house was about twelve feet across and long and winding. In the winter, it was bad and icy. I refused to drive it on bad weather days. He would get so mad. One day I could not get it down the driveway for fear of going over the cliff. He made me get out halfway down when I froze up and drove it on down. He also managed to drive it off the driveway a little bit once and got it stuck hanging on the hill. He was by himself and called for the warehouse man. When the warehouse man got up the drive, there, the owner, was on the ground, down the hill, yelling for help. The warehouse man managed to drag him up in the mud to safety. They had to call for a wrecker. The owner told the warehouse man that he saved his life, could never repay him. We tried not to smile about this, but the owner always thought he was the toughest and was very bullheaded.

On our way back from San Diego, my ear blew out completely, just went completely dead. When we got back, the owner suggested I see the doctor. I was reluctant but needed to keep peace. So it turned out the doctor said I needed a tube put in it, and he would do it. The owner said, "He is such a good doctor, let him do it." So I did. He laid me on the table and strapped me in and forced that tube in. It was weird that no fluid came out. The doctor said it would in time. Well, it never quite did, and more on that later, which, if I had known, my suspicions would have been right on this man.

Now Klein was one of the owner's best friends. I might have talked about him earlier. But there is more to tell. He had been with the owner for over fifty years. He lived two hours away, Jewish, had been in the service during WWII, and that was where they met. He was a salesman and was always a pleasure to see. All the women knew how handsome he was. He and the owner would go to lunch, and then he would be on his way back. The owner kept a picture of him and his brothers in his office. The owner and I would go visit him when they both quit driving. I became close to him, and he had a daughter living in Israel. Her husband was Shavis.

Now this story gets sad and twisted.

Life is taking a toll on the owner. His aging process is not being kind at all, and he missed his wife badly. He was becoming agitated all the time. His hired help was not good. One was not even supposed to be a caretaker. She was just there for the drugs. The one he liked the most eventually stole his credit cards while he slept.

I went into his office one day, and he showed me a receipt from a grocery store. It had pork chops on it and beer. Well, being Jewish, he never bought pork chops and beer. It was in the middle of the night when bought. So the best caretaker turned out to be a credit-card thief.

None of these caretakers came to his funeral, by the way, after years of service.

I then got invited to a bar mitzvah. I said, "Sure, I will take you." I was excited again, not sure what to wear. It was fun. The songs, the

82   PAM CROFT

talking, everything was great. The looks I got, not so much. Never before had he called me his friend when asked who I was. This was a special moment. Usually, it was a worker or caretaker. The food was excellent once again.

So the meetings we had to take over the stores dwindled away. This was so sad. The owner thought of a new approach to this situation. He would change his will. He would find a new lawyer and have it drawn up. He told the warehouse man and I would have to drive him to this lawyer, not knowing why. The warehouse man drove him as well.

As this was being done, the doctor's history with us is not pretty. When the owner's wife died, he came to the house and started opening drawers and looking through everything while the owner was sick in bed. He asked me and the warehouse man where her jewelry was. We said we did not know what he was talking about. He kept looking, tearing up the drawers. He also messed with the owner's medicines. The owner trusted him up to a point. When the owner was in the hospital for the third time, he finally was told his medicine had hurt his kidneys. That was the first moment the owner realized the doctor had messed with them. The owner called the rabbi and cried to him about this. The rabbi did not believe him and said to settle down, he would come.

The doctor and his wife came to the hospital and acted shocked at these allegations. The owner told me in front of them, "Someone stinks in here and needs to leave." They left, and the rabbi came and told him that they were trying to kill him.

The rabbi, the next few weeks, talked with the owner about this and convinced him that the doctor did not try to kill him. The owner forgave the doctor, and he was back in. This was when I started really knowing what this bad doctor could do.

So as the owner gets better over time, I still had to drive him all the time now. The bad part of this was whenever someone would call him, it would come through the speakers. The doctor would call quite often and always seemed to know when I was driving.

I was still trying to understand the connection and hold this man had on the owner. He always seemed to know what was going on. They were not related, but rumors spread that he was the owner's son. I do not believe this. However, on a phone conversation one day, the owner did call him *bubala*. I looked it up when I got home and was not happy with what I found. It said someone very close, possibly a grandmother or some other person of closeness. Then I was upset because this man was really getting my suspicions up.

One day I was fixing the owner lunch at his house when up comes the doctor. I tried to keep busy in the kitchen when the doctor told me to come into the dining room. The doctor asked me many questions about my family. Of course, I answered them in a nice way, trying to be cordial, did not want to piss anyone off.

After the doctor left, the owner scolded me for answering his questions and told me not to get too cozy with him. I just shrugged and said OK, even though my feelings of suspicion came back again.

All the relatives were calling more because they knew he was going downhill. He knew why also. They wanted to come visit him, and he strongly told each and every one of them no. I asked him why not let them come. He said if they come, they will not leave and will not let me or any of the store people come up ever again to the house or see him. This was really getting crazy.

I learned that the Swiss banks had many a Holocaust victim's family money in it. The owner was aware of this too. So the main thing before he would pass away was to go get this large sum of money that was there for him. That was the stipulation. You had to go get it. His father had a hosiery and sock store. Whether that is where all the money came from, I don't know, but I do know the doctor knew of this money also. And there you go, the trip was in the making, even though the owner was frail and eighty-seven or eighty-eight, give or take. I understand him wanting to do this, but I was worried. I was scared to go but wasn't on the list anyway to go.

Who do you think went? Of course, the bad doctor.

I was to take them up to the airport and see them off. I did not talk the whole trip up. I was slowly hating this man, the doctor. The trip was extended also. Switzerland first, then Israel. The owner wanted to visit there one more time. He had many friends there and loved it there. Now I was more worried than ever, but glad I was not invited on this trip as I would have worried about his health so far away.

After I dropped them off, I was going to go to a cabin with some coworkers for some rest and fun. Before the cabin, though, I was in charge of washing the owner's car and vacuuming it. The owner did say I could stay at his house if I wanted to.

I went to the surplus store, which I am still managing in all this. We had new people working there, and one of the girls was with Vern, the other worker. The new girl is Lisa and was a great asset to the store. She too was trying to understand this whole situation with my life. We are still good friends to this day, and we travel a lot.

So I grabbed Vern and asked him to come with me to the carwash, and I would buy them lunch. Vern is a good friend also to this day. He still helps me with situations. He was a great listener during this, and I will be forever thankful.

We pulled into the carwash and vacuumed the car. Then I pulled around to the automatic port. I don't use these much because they make me nervous trying to hit the rail. I have been known to miss. This Lexus is brand new, and here I am, trying this. Sure enough, I missed! I missed so bad that it dragged the car along with a horrible scraping noise and then stopping halfway through not moving anymore whatsoever. The carwash itself was stuck on waxing the car.

I was screaming to Vern, "What do we do?"

"Stay calm," he said in his manner when someone shows up shutting the wax off and guiding me on through slowly until I scrape myself out the door.

So Vern got out and came around to drive it through the right way to get the wax scum off. It never did come off. So now I am panicking badly. It looked horrible. Instead of a sharp gray, it was a blurry white car.

I told Vern I was done with this whole mess.

Vern said, "No way, I can't walk away now."

I said, "I suppose," and took Vern back to the store. I went to get the warehouse man and begged him to fix the car. He said yes and worked on it a long time, buffing that wax off.

I worked at the store while the owner was gone, and it felt good to be back. Then I went on the trip with my coworkers. It was fun. Unfortunately, the owner called my phone and said they flew back early and I needed to come to the airport to get them. Furiously, I said I was on a horseback ride and at a cabin, and I would not. "Call the warehouse man." I was glad he was back safely but not happy about interrupting my trip when I knew he was not due back yet. I am proud of myself to this day.

Now he was getting slower all the time and more cantankerous. He had this new lawyer making up his new will. He was in and out of the hospital all the time. I noticed something weird about this. The numbers on his arm for Auschwitz camp were always coming up in his life, his telephone number, his address, his room numbers, when admitted to the hospital. I asked him one day if he ever noticed this. He said, "Yes, of course, I do, and it is OK." More on this later.

I took him to the cemetery a few times to see his wife. I told him this made me feel strange, and he said, "I want you to know where I will be, so you can come see me." Again, I cringed at this. The headstone for his wife was not done yet. We made many trips to the headstone people over this. He also made it a point for me to know how he wanted their headstone to look like. He argued the color of the granite, the writing on the granite, with the people many times. He said, "For ten thousand, they should be listening to me." Finally, it was done, and of course, the granite was too light, but he agreed to it. So now I knew where this would be in the future.

So now we have the warehouse man taking the owner to the big city to finalize the new will. It still needed changes, of course. Driving him, he would tell me, "When I die, the first thing you need to do is get a lawyer." I hated when he would say this, as I did not like to think he was leaving us, ever. I had grown to love this man. He would tell the office girl every so often, "The angel of death did not come and see me last night, or you would be a very rich woman today!"

The relatives were swarming more and more, the doctor closer than ever. Every time he had a scheduled meeting with the new lawyer, he was in the hospital. One time the weather was very bad, and the new lawyer did not try to come, so again, no signing. This makes me wonder about this lawyer now too. The lawyer would call the phone and ask me to set up another day it needs to get done. One was scheduled on a Sunday, and the lawyer called and said he did not want to work that day. I think we were up to four times cancelling on this very important signing of the new will. The last and final scheduled day was when the owner passed away. No new will signature.

"Who is this new lawyer? And what is he doing?" we all asked at the store.

It was the night of the Superbowl, and I was watching it at home with friends and family when I got a call from the manager of the big store. The owner was having trouble breathing and wanted to go to the hospital. The manager wanted me to meet them out there. I went and remembered he had a strange rattle the day before. I was worried. His spirits were strange, not himself. They got him to a room, and I stayed with him until three o'clock that morning. He ate half a sandwich and just did not feel good, very agitated. I told him I needed to go home and get some sleep because I had a doctor's appointment in the morning, and then I would come to the hospital. I said if he wanted to go to a different hospital, I would take him, or if he wanted to go home, I would do that. Over the years, we have been known to discharge him without a form because he was tired of the hospital. He said OK.

I called one of the caretakers that next morning on my way to the doctor and asked her if she had seen him. She said no, which made me mad, and she said he had a very bad night. I said OK and hung up and called the owner's cell phone. He answered and asked where I was and when would I get there. He was ready to leave. I asked if he was alone, and he said the warehouse guy was with him.

I said good and that I would be there shortly to do whatever he wanted.

He said, "No, turn the car around now and get here."

I said, "I will be there in an hour. I love you. Goodbye."

I got to the doctor's office and waited. I waited and waited and waited. *What is wrong here?* I asked myself. I was so fidgety and hated waiting. Finally, he came in and apologized for being late. I now knew I should have not gone. Or there was a reason for this wait from the good Lord.

I left the doctors and sped my way back to town and straight to the hospital. When I got to the right floor, I noticed the warehouse man in the hallway with the store manager. Instantly, I knew what was up. They told me I was ten minutes too late, and they were working on him.

I did not know what to do. I sat down and cried and was so mad at myself and the doctor who was late.

I asked the warehouse man what happened. He said the owner was up and sat on the bed and wanted his legs rubbed. The warehouse man rubbed them with lotion, and when the owner turned to lie down, he looked shocked and died. One of the doctors who saw him that morning said his kidneys were shutting down, and the owner refused to get dialysis, so there was no hope. Again, no new will signed or ever would be.

Reality was my life would have a major change in it, and it would be without my hero.

When they told us we could go in, we did. I instantly went to his bed and touched his face and kissed his forehead. He looked at peace now. Hopefully, he would be with his long lost family. I held him. Just then the bad doctor came in and went to a corner and gasped and cried. Whether he really was crying or not, who knows? He then turned around and told me I was not supposed to be touching the body. Jewish traditions are not to touch the body, and he would be covering him up now. I said, "Oh well, I did what I needed to do." The doctor then covered him up and sat down.

We were waiting for the funeral home to come, and they were about an hour away. We—the doctor, the warehouse man, the big store manager, and me—all sat in silence. This was it. The doctor got this stupid idea that we all should tell a little story about the owner while we wait for the funeral home.

When the funeral home people arrived, they took him away without any words to us the workers for the store, made us feel what was coming real fast. The doctor had total control of the conversation. We were just observers.

We went to the store from there and told everyone what has happened. Then the doctor wanted all three of us to go up to the owner's house for a minute. What the hell was this? Even worse, he asked to ride up with me in my jeep. What the hell again? What could I say to this? We got in my jeep, and he asked me, "What year is this vehicle?" I tell him I am so sick from the day and he says isn't it funny we are talking about your car when the owner just passed away. Now I knew what a sick fuck I would be dealing with.

We got up to the house, and again, he was rummaging through it. We just stood there like idiots. He finally stopped and asked me, "How would you feel about me being your boss?"

WHAT THE HELL AGAIN! My hero just died, and he was totally crazy on what he was doing.

I said, "No way. There is only one boss for me, and he just passed away."

He replied, "Think about it."

After that, he said one more thing to all of us, that if we ever wanted to quit the store we had, see him first. Do not ever leave without telling him.

When we left the house, we let the doctor go and the three of us went across the street to get a drink. We did not talk much, just sat there sad and shocked. We were worried about what was coming next. We were just so sad about this day. When we got to the bar, everyone said, "Hey, it's the store people." We did not know what to say. So we said what needed to be said about the owner. This town was going to be in shock and sad. I just knew my Februarys were never going to be the same.

When I got home, my husband was very worried about how I was doing. He knew I had just taken a big loss in life.

I did not go back to the store that day. The other two did to spread the word. I went home feeling empty and knew life was changing. People asked me if I was OK and how I was doing a lot. My family was wonderful to me and gave me space.

My mom's sister lives in Florida and was in her eighties when this happened. I would visit her once a year, and my trip was for next week after the owner's death. I already had my plane ticket before this happened and knew this would be a good way to get over some of the shock. My aunt lived in a condo all by herself, and I knew she would take care of me and baby me.

As you know, Jewish people need to be buried by sundown or within twenty-four hours. Well, we could not do this as all the relatives needed to fly here. It was held four days later, I believe.

I went back to work the day after the owner's passing. I must say I just wanted to stay drunk all the time because that was how I handled my parents' deaths. I usually drank hard for six months and then let up. The store was in an uproar. The worst thing was when I went in, the manager of the big store had already moved into the owner's office and was now using his cellphone. He had just gotten a new company car a year before this. The owner always made sure he had one, along with a gas card to use all the time.

I thought this was very aggressive of him to do this. He acted very goofy. I realize the owner was like a dad to him, but where was he when we needed him to take the store over earlier, and where was he when we needed help taking turns caretaking? Nowhere to be found, that's where.

I also noticed all the Picasso prints that were on the owner's wall were gone. I asked the manager who took those, and sure enough, he said the doctor came in and grabbed them. I still wonder if the relatives know this.

It was a tough bad day, and all I knew I was ready to drink. I could not stay there long. Throwing up could happen if I stayed.

The manager called a meeting to the front of the store. He closed the store for a few days. Everyone came to the front of the store. The manager started talking about how the store would be ran, starting with him and then on down the line. The assistant manager was furious over this, and these two hated each other. The assistant manager said there should be a vote, and the manager said no. It was as if our parents had died and the children were trying to figure this out.

Then the manager said, "I would like to take this opportunity to thank Pam," which is me, "for all the hard years she put in taking such good care of the owner." Then everyone clapped. I did not care about these nice words or the clapping. I just wanted the owner to walk through those doors and everything be the same. I left right after this to go you know what.

When the owner's wife passed, we carpooled up to the funeral home from the store because it was about a forty-minute ride. The owner had his main caretaker at night to be with him, which was fine with me because at that time, I did not know what to say to him. He also looked so bad and sickly.

When the owner passed, I rode with the warehouse man and a few others. It was bad. Not a lot of people came. Whoever did the obituary made it about three lines' worth. All the relatives were there and wanted me to sit up front with them which made me feel good. I chose not to. Of course, the doctor did. After the funeral, we went to the synagogue and ate food. This was when it first happened. When I say this, I am talking about the beginning of the meaning of "When I die, you better get a lawyer." But of course, I did not think about that then.

The new lawyer came up to all of us at our tables while we were eating. He announced that he was the owner's lawyer. He was asking each of our name. However, with me, he said, "Who is Pam?" I said that would be me. He held his hand out to shake my hand and said it his big lawyer way, "Pam, I am so sorry for what did not get done in the end." I was shocked, did not know what to say, should have said "tell me what the new will said" but didn't. Everyone just looked at us with shock.

I noticed the doctor who was supposed to look after us like his own personal flock of sheep had slid out the door and left.

So now begins the horrible drama. The doctor was a coexecutor, along with cousin Tim in Tennessee, who is old. The beneficiary was the Holocaust Museum in Israel. The will was the old one, and a lot of the people in it were dead. The new one probably was shredded fast since no signature was acquired.

The doctor went up and ravaged through the house for sure. When we went up to clean the refrigerator, the house was a mess. He sure went through it well. Poor Tim in Tennessee probably lost out. The doctor would never ever clean this house. For six years, he left the sheets and towels that were used that same bad night on the bed. We found cleaners for him, and he never let them come. He never helped with the owner's health, so how did he get to be coexecutor? He just kept telling the warehouse man to do the cleaning, and the warehouse man was just as upset as all of us and said no.

After the funeral, I was off to my aunt's house, anxious to get away. I was on my second day there when I got a text message from one of the caretakers. It was not a nice one, and she said I was nothing but a bitch. This caretaker was the one who never came to the hospital to see him or the funeral. She said something about she should have been the one in the paper, not me.

I called the store and asked was there something in the paper about the owner. The manager said yes. He did an interview with the local paper about the owner and the store. He said he also put me in it as a great friend and caretaker. The paper wanted to talk to me, but the manager said I was away. My husband read it to me when I called him. It was a beautiful article, a great tribute to the owner. I wish I could have been there to help with it. I felt honored to be in it. I texted the caretaker back and said, "I am in Florida and had nothing to do with that article. My manager did the interview. You can apologize to me anytime, and where were you when we needed you most?" No reply.

I did run into her at a restaurant a year later and asked her, "Where is my apology?"

She said, "Just let it go." I walked away.

Florida was great, and it did help some. My aunt babied me greatly. When I got back, things were worse than ever at the store.

I still was trying to manage my store best as I could. I just could not stay very long at a time knowing that the owner wasn't going to pull up for me to drive him or call me to come up to the house to help him. It was too hard. I never did put myself back on the schedule.

The meetings were starting to happen. Five of us were to be in them: me, the manager, hardware lady, assistant manager who also ran sporting goods, office lady and the manager from southern store. All of us different from each other and now five people to argue with.

The doctor was the first one to call. I had my questions lined up also, while the others were just staring like spots on the wall. The doctor said things were going to run like usual, but we needed to go to the bank to get a loan in our names to buy the stores. Otherwise, they would be shut down. It would have to be a million-dollar loan. My first question was, "Could I buy the store that I ran by itself?"

He said, "No, the owner did not want to split it up."

My second question was "Should we go get a lawyer."

The doctor said, "No way. If the beneficiary in Israel finds out about this, they would close it up immediately. This way, we can run it awhile until we get a loan."

I fucking believed him. He said we have to let the sleeping dog lie.

So my husband had his suspicions also about who was making money now. The accountant who the store had was somewhat crooked to.

The doctor's meetings were every Tuesday around noon. His office in our town was open that day. The first couple of meetings were tense. He always would manage to make a comment to me in front of everybody. His actions meant he was worried about me getting a lawyer. I am sure of this now. He said at one meeting, "I know now what Pam would look like as a man." We all stopped and stared at him, waiting for where he was going with this. I did not reply or give in to this. He said there was a guy that worked at the bank he just went to, and he thought it was me. Then realized it was my son working there.

I did not laugh as the others did. I just stared at him still and shrugged with a smile. I was not happy with this comment from him. The next time, after the meeting, I was out on the floor looking away, and he came up behind me and gave my neck a few squeezes as he walked by and left. This made me feel very creepy.

He never did much at these meetings, only to say, "Hurry up and get your loan, time is running out." What a liar. None of us wanted to invest in this shit arrangement. We always said, "Who was buying the most?" It would be hardware and sporting goods. Hardware, so the south store would have extras and sporting goods so the assistant manager could buy all the knives he wanted and candy. So much candy it would mold before selling it. The assistant manager was always monitored before the owner died. Now he was free to do what he wanted and would not listen to the manager.

There fights got worse and worse. The manager did try to advertise more and spent a bundle of money on it and got ridiculed for this.

So the assistant manager was scheming to get the manager fired eventually so he could run the store himself.

Then once every month or two, the accountant would visit us. He had about an hour and a half drive. He would give us statements that would never make sense. How do I know this? My husband happens to be a CPA and runs a credit union. Never in the last five years of this did we ever see a true statement that was accurate. My husband would write down the questions to ask him, and he always squirmed his way out of it. The others just sat there and watched this bullshit session. He got paid big bucks too. He ended up hating me also. I tried to explain to the coworkers what he was doing, but no one would listen.

The financial statements were of little value because inventory was never updated. So over and over, the same questions were asked and never quite answered right. Something funny here again.

So now I have the accountant and the doctor making me furious. The lawyer made an appearance once in a while but nothing worthwhile.

Tim, the coexecutor, came once, and I talked with him since I knew him, but he seemed like he just didn't care about what was going on, very distant with me.

I started getting phone calls at the store I ran from relatives and friends. The first one was from the cousins in California. They asked how I was doing with losing him. They said they were very sad, and the next thing was, has any money been distributed yet to anyone?

WHAT! I said I have no clue and sorry. They said they were just wondering because they had not heard anything. I said they had to go back to an old will, and they did not sound happy when they hung up. That was the last time I spoke with them.

The next one was from his longtime friend Monty, who came every Thursday to see him and once worked at the store. It was his daughter who made the call. She asked, "How are you doing?"

I thought, *Uh-oh, here we go.* I said, "Fine."

She asked if I knew of any money being distributed that the owner told Monty he would be getting quite a lot of money when he died. Again, I had to say the new will did not get signed, so I did not know. Never heard from her again on that subject.

We were all waiting for the unveiling of the headstone. I waited three months before pressuring the assistant manager to get the doctor to get the headstone done. He was up his behind anyway, so I figured he could take care of this. Finally, after another month, it was done and ready for the unveiling. There were about six of us who went to it, along with the doctor and Tim. Monty came as well.

We were all standing there not knowing what they do for this when the doctor asked me to help him unveil it. I said, "No, thank you," but he insisted. So I did, and glad I did. He also offered me a little headstone with that, and I declined on that. It is still there today.

After the unveiling, Monty came up to me and asked, "Where is the money that I am supposed to get?"

I said, "I have no idea and am sorry about this." I told him to go talk to the doctor about it, and he got so mad with the whole situation. He hugged me and left.

The final call I received was from the salesman who lived two hours away and was his good friend. He put his son-in-law on the phone. His name was Shaver, and he wanted to know where his father-in-law's money was. He told me he was coming to our town and wanted a meeting with me. He was very hard to understand with his accent. He said he would call again when he got there. I hung up feeling very concerned and a little scared. Why were all these people coming at me?

I went over to the big store and told them what had happened, and they did not seem to care. Only the warehouse man said he would help take care of him.

It had been about seven months now since the owner had passed away. Not feeling any better about the store or our meetings, I asked the office girl who had worked there thirty years now if she would go with me to a lawyer to see if we could get the new will reinstated. We all were told not possible by the new lawyer in the beginning of this. We knew the new will would let us keep the stores. The owner most likely was giving us our stores we wanted in the new will.

She said yes she would go.

I found a good lawyer in town and made an appointment. We were so nervous but did not care. We wanted justice done.

We told the lawyer about the Holocaust Museum in Israel, not knowing about his passing. We told them about the new will not getting signed. We told them everything. Looking very somber and sad, he said we actually had six months to fight the new will, but unfortunately, it was past this time. We started crying. We knew the owner's new lawyer knew this but refused to tell us. We left feeling very empty.

Shaver called again, and this time he was in town. He was staying at a local hotel and wanted me to meet him at his room. I said no, we could meet at a restaurant. He said fine. I got the warehouse man, and we went and met him.

Shaver was a very angry man. He explained over and over about his father-in-law was to receive and huge amount of money from the owner. He demanded that I get a lawyer and fight this. I tried to explain to him that I already did this, but he refused to believe me. I think he thought I received a bunch of money. So he gave me his cell phone number and said he was going back to his father-in-law's and would find a lawyer for me. He wanted me to pay for the lawyer also. We said goodbye.

About a month later, he called again. He said he has found a lawyer and was coming down to see me. I said, "Don't do that, it won't work." He came anyway and wanted me again to meet him at his room. I said no, and again, we went to the restaurant with the warehouse man as well. He did not bring the lawyer but he brought all the information on him. I told him how sorry I was, but there was nothing we could do. He went to the store and tried to tell the manager there what we needed to do before it was too late. The manager told him it was already too late, and that was all there was to it. He left, and I never heard from him again.

After all this, I decided I was going to write all the legal people for the estate a letter to which would say I want to purchase the little store and made them an offer. No reply from anyone. I would send it periodically over the next six years. Never a reply.

I had to visit the doctor every so often because if you remember, he put a tube in my ear and needed to see if it had fallen out yet. Each time I went, it was nerve-racking. I hated him at this point. He would follow me out after barely looking in my ear, and when I would write a check, he would come up in front of everyone and tear it up. I kept telling him I did not want to owe him anything. He knew all that I had seen him do over the years. I am sure not to mention some nice Picasso prints.

It was getting near fall, and still, I was not working much and still wetting my whistle maybe three times a week.

I was trying to feel better about this whole mess. The manager was wasting his time and the store's money arguing with the assistant manager every day. The assistant manager was bound and determined to get rid of him and slowly was convincing the doctor to do it.

My coworkers and I were about to have a night out one night. I went into town a little early, maybe midafternoon. I had just walked into a store when, all of a sudden, I had an earache come along that I had never had before. It was in the opposite ear of the one that had a tube in it. I had to stop and just stand there, not knowing what to do. It went down my throat and then back up. I got my cell phone out and called the doctor to see if he was in. He was not there that day, but his partner was. I pleaded to get in to see him and told them I was in such pain. They agreed to see me.

This is so hard for me to write.

The doctor examined me and looked a little worried. He asked, "When was the last time you saw the doctor who put your tube in?"

I said, "Last month."

He asked, "Did he look down your throat or up your nose?"

I said, "No, he never does that." I said I was sure it was my sinuses as it was getting near fall of this very bad year.

He said, "You need to come back and see him when he gets in because there is a spot on your adenoid not looking good." He said he probably would want a biopsy.

I was never so shocked. I said, "I am not ever going to come back to this doctor ever." I left that day and took my files with me.

I found an ENT in a town down the road. He examined me as well and, sure enough, said I needed a biopsy. By this time, my other ear was not hearing well. I said, "OK, and could you put a tube in my other ear as well?"

Now I was really nervous because surely the doctor would not want me dead too.

I got through the surgery, and my husband greeted me in the recovery room. I was all happy because I could finally hear pretty good.

My husband started crying and said, "Pam, you have cancer."

I just smiled and said, "That is fine, I can hear, and we will take care of the cancer."

I was then realizing what a horrific year I was having. I just had turned fifty years old. The owner had made it to my birthday. That was a big request that I gave him. I turned fifty in December of the year before he passed away. He passed in February. Now this horrific year was getting worse. I had cancer.

My mind was racing with the doctor not catching it in my nose. After all, he is an ENT. He had taken care of my ear problem for three years and not once noticed the tumor on my adenoid. So it was seemingly more and more real that he did want certain people to die. People who might hurt him in life mostly because of money.

This was a slow-growing cancer, so that was the good part. Unfortunately, it had made my lymph nodes swollen in my neck, so now it automatically became stage 3. The procedure for this was not to remove the tumor because of the location but seven weeks of radiation daily, except for weekends, chemo once a week; then at the end of seven weeks, wear a fanny pack at home that would distribute chemo for a few days. I was supposed to do the fanny pack three times, but it was so bad I could only do it once.

When I went to the store to tell them, they were all shocked. I did not hold back about the doctor missing my cancer.

When the doctor was in one day at the store, I told him what was going to be happening. I had to grab him as he was rushing out the door. I don't know if anyone had told him or not. I told him that I had cancer on the adenoid and would be getting hard treatments. He did his normal shocking, surprised look that everyone knew as a lie and said, "Why are you not seeing me?"

I said, "No, I am going elsewhere."

He said, "You will be fine," and left.

So I started my treatments, and yes, it was tough. The worry was bad enough, but the side effects were bad. I was told that I only had so much weight to lose until they would insert a feeding tube, that my mouth sores would be bad. They sure were right. I could not eat. I did not work much either. I did not want to be around people because of germs. I lost twenty-five pounds from it. They threatened me again about the tube, so I just kept with my special recipe of soaked Rice Krispies. I was determined to win this. No feeding tube.

From the side effects of this, I was madder and madder at the doctor. He came into the store one day when I happened to be visiting. He came over after a month of treatments and asked, "How was are you doing?"

I replied, "What do you care?"

He said, "I do," and walked away.

I just figured he was seeing if I was near death yet, if his plan was working.

I caught him in the parking lot when he was leaving and said I would like to say something to him. He said OK. I started off with "I know you are trying to kill me—"

He stopped me and said, "Don't ever say that."

I said, "I just did, and you should have seen this spot on my adenoid after three years of treating me. Your partner caught it in one visit. Your partner saved my life." I then said, "You don't have to worry about me taking you to court. I am not doing that. But I want you to promise me you will always check adenoids from now on." He agreed to this and left.

When I finished treatments, I took a gift certificate to the doctor's partner and told him how thankful I was for him that day. To this day, I send him a card every year, thanking him for saving me.

So about five months after treatments, I was cleared and getting my strength back. I went back to work, hoping to be able to do better at the store.

That was a mistake. It was worse than ever—more fighting, more spending, more meetings that did not make sense. We hired our own accountant to try to help us. This man was not the best either, and my husband had seen this also. You couldn't do much when things just didn't add up. There was no way we were ever going to get a loan.

The assistant manager was worse than ever on scheming to get the big guy out that was above him. The manager knew this and took precautions and went and got a van just in case they took his company car away. The manager was not recovering well from the owner's death. He did not show authority and sales were down. He just did not seem like he knew what he was doing and was tired of getting shot down by others for his efforts. He had said he has been there for forty years and was tired.

The manager was the only one from the store who called me every day to see how I was doing when I was sick.

We all received big raises when the owner died. I am sure it was so none of us left and the store would fail. They were all money-hungry.

Each week, when the doctor would still come in, I could not even look at him at this point. People were starting to call him their boss. I would tell them there was no way this man would ever be my boss. They would say I had no choice at this point.

But I did.

It had been about three years since the owner passed, and I went into work. I went to my store, and the manager was in the back, wanting to talk to me. I walked back, and he said he had to go. I asked where. He said he had an envelope on his desk, and it said he had to leave for good. I was devastated. This man was always on my side.

I asked, "When will you let me know how you are doing?"

He said, "As soon as the gag order is lifted." So I figured they bought him out.

I said, "Let's go tell the warehouse man."

We walked over to a warehouse to tell him. The warehouse man did not act surprised. He just said, "Sorry to hear this, and come visit us." I knew he knew what was going on.

I told the manager goodbye and he said he would let me know. It has been eight years now and still have not heard from him.

I went back in the store, and there was the assistant manager grinning from ear to ear. I told him that this whole thing was just awful. The assistant manager had already taken the company cell phone. He was trying to tell me how to order merchandise from now on when I walked away.

The next day, not feeling good at all, I went in to work. There, in the break room, was the assistant manager telling the five of us how we were going to be splitting the manager's salary up. We all would get raises equaling $20 an hour, except for the woman who ran the south store. She already made enough, so she does not get any.

I was just sick again listening to this. I said I couldn't do this anymore: the bad doctor, the unfairness of this money. We were supposed to be using that money to buy the store. The assistant manager did not care, and I said, "I am done here." I clocked out and left for good.

The doctor called my cell phone later that day. I forgot his rule about telling him if I were to leave. Fuck that. He left me a message saying that he had heard I quit and was not happy. I had full authority of my store, and he did not understand, that I should call him.

I called him and said all there was to say about the assistant manager, and he said I could come back any time I wanted to.

Just a few facts on the assistant manager.

I worked with him for about twenty years. During this time, he usually left me alone but still jealous of the little store doing so well. He knew I was close to the owner, so the assistant manager became my good friend during that time. As a person, he was somewhat sarcastic at times but did have a sense of humor about him.

He loved attention and would arrange meetings and then would not talk at them.

On the business side, he would order freely, and then when it would come in, let it sit in the warehouse. He always claimed he was saving it for Christmas, even though it was only October. He would order a few things for me but take forever to do it. My sales would suffer from this.

He would be on the computer all day.

He would make you wait in the morning for your money bag, even though people would be standing outside the door waiting.

He lost one of my biggest customers one day when they bought something for their car, and when he went out to try it, it did not fit. He brought it back in to return it, and the assistant manager charged him a restocking fee. The merchandise never left the parking lot. My customer never came back.

So this was a big reason for leaving also. I loved my job, but there was no way I was going to have this person think he was now running it. I had to leave. I could not work in this environment after just getting well myself, and it came as a financial cost to me.

Before the owner died, we did have some good times, and he was a very good person. When he saw me come in the store after I had left, he called me trouble.

I am sorry to say he did pass away seven years after the owner's death. It bothered me bad. He never came out of his house much and did not take care of himself. This was after the store had closed.

So before I left, the warehouse man had been trying to go up to the owner's house to clean it out some. It was obvious none of the executors was going to do this or the lawyer. They had no respect for the owner. If he knew this, I can only imagine what he would do. I often wonder what he would have done had he been alive when I was diagnosed with cancer. I did not know I had the cancer when I was trying to take care of him. That was why my ear blew out in the first place two years before when I got the tube put in. The only thing I noticed was my energy level was very low. I thought it was from juggling everything and stress. I would need to take a nap up at his house. Thank goodness, he needed one too. I am sure the doctor would have had many troubles from him if the owner knew what had happened.

I feel as though he did know from heaven about this. I noticed when I went for my first day of radiation and chemotherapy treatments that they gave me a wrist band the number sequence right away. This is how I know to this day he was with me. Seven weeks of treatments with mouth sores and all is what I went through so I kept looking at the numbers to help me.

The warehouse man had been bringing more items down from the house. He always asked me if I wanted to go up with him, and I would say no, it was too hard for me. The owner's bed was still not made from his last night alive. That was two years past at this point.

One day he brought picture albums down to the store. In at least ten of the photo albums they took trips, the owner, his wife, and relatives, you name it, they were there. They were wonderful, and I could not believe no one wanted them in the family! How could a man of this power not have anyone blood-related not care?

We called one of the relatives in Washington State to see if she was interested. She had come to the house ever since she was a little girl, and the owner just loved her. She was spunky. She came before he got really sick and was still allowing visitors. I liked her right away. She wanted to hear stories of the past, and this was good because I got to hear them. She was the one who invited me to sit with her at the funeral.

She got so excited when we offered her the picture books. She could not understand what happened with this whole mess. We tried to explain it all to her. She was so sorry for the mess, but there was nothing she could do. We knew this and said anything else she wanted from the house, she could have because no one wanted anything. The next day we sent her the books not before I could grab a couple of good pictures of the owner and his wife on vacation. The owner was so happy looking in these photos.

During the owner's bad days, he would tell me there was a picture of him as a toddler that was so picture-perfect. "I was a beautiful toddler," he would tell me, "and could you please try to find it so I could show it you?" I searched and searched for days, never coming up with it. Of course, I found it in the books buried after he had passed, and he was correct in what he said. He was a beautiful toddler. Yes, indeed, I have this picture hidden away in my treasure chest.

I also found a poem in these books that I kept. He had cut it out from a newspaper many years ago. It is now old and yellow paper but still readable. It is a poem about not being able to help his mother during the Holocaust, the sweetness of her face, and how she would never hurt a blade of grass. Why could he not save her? It showed the true sadness he felt his whole life, along with hundreds more sons who lost their mothers to the Nazis. This man still lived in hell, even though he survived.

Even though I had quit the store, I still called every day to get the scoop on this crooked, bad situation. I also went to probate on the web and would watch everything that would happen, from meetings to payments to when the store would close.

Things were not getting any better. They fired my friend from my store after picking on her since I had left. They kept Vern, and a new girl was running the store. Prices went up, and I am not sure how they did. I do know they did not hesitate to fill the store way more than needed. I figured it must be fun to spend money that is not yours, with no limits whatsoever. The idea of them buying the store was long gone, so now how long could it run like this?

It was a total of six years.

I checked probate every day, not much change in it. They would pay their fees and then let it run for another year, someone making money and knowing they were screwing someone like a beneficiary. The assistant manager was loving running the store, even though it was doing terrible, lots and lots of candy to be bought, hardware overflowing, my store overflowing, a big outdoor line of clothing was brought in, tons of it.

I had gone and gotten several new jobs. I was too young not to. First was as a receptionist at a nursing facility. I learned everything and did like this job. The people running it were a bunch of fakes, I felt. They were snooty and acted like they had tons of money. Things were bad after a while. People who were staying there knew me from the past and always were nice and willing to learn about the store. They were getting less and less attention due to low staffing. This bothered me bad. So I left. It was a few months later, a new company came in and took over firing all the people who were running it.

The next job would be a forty-minute job to an arena that had ice hockey and concerts. I was a ticket taker. I really enjoyed this job also. I got to see so many performers. I worked there about a year. One time I did not get a break for seven hours, and when I finally got one, the food that we were getting that day was all ate up. I also had to pay for my parking too. I left soon after this.

The next job was at a fudge company down at a local outdoor flea market that had a diner and putt putt in it. It was a very busy place. This woman with five children just bought it. She was trying to teach me it all but not the fudge-making part. I loved this job. I filled the candy and coffee every day. And the fudge was delicious. It even had a huge coffee machine that would bake the beans.

After six months, the owner was getting a little bitchy. Her kids were always sick, and she would bring them into the shop. She did not know which end was up half the time. She had a tip jar at the counter, which I hated because I did not want to be tipped. She told me the tips went to her church. One weekend that I worked by myself, we were packed all day. It was summer, and people were on vacation. The tip jar was overflowing. I was not happy with it. So I took it away on the shelf. Never did I get a "thank you" for the tips, only a "wow, that jar has never been that far." So I knew what I was capable of doing with a business.

I often went and looked at spots to rent for my own military store. I owned a dog tag machine that I had bought before the owner died. He disapproved of this machine, said it was a waste of money. I did not care, I loved making them. I was not sure about running a business all the time. My time was valuable ever since the cancer, always wondering if or when it could come back. I still worry about this.

So I was at this fudge shop one day and noticed a note she put on the counter for me. It said, "Please do not cut the fudge to where you leave small pieces. Take a broom and go outside and get the cobweb off the light." After six months, this pissed me off. First of all, when I ran my store, if I saw a cobweb, I got rid of it on my own. Second, I had been cutting fudge for six months, and now she says something. So I just threw the paper away and did not do any of that. She came into the store one hour later. I looked at her and said, "You couldn't have just told me about these things?"

She said, "I did not think I was coming in, so I wrote you a note."

I then said, I am not going to do any of this because it just was not working out."

She said, "OK, that is fine then. You can go."

Wow, evidently, her plan worked. What a bitch. She sold her store out, even though the people who were older practically gave her it and took the money and ran.

I realized then that I would not get another job. Everyone would joke about how long I would stay at another job. I realized I did not want another boss. I wanted to be my own boss. I wanted the owner to be my boss only, and that was never going to happen again.

It was a good thing I worked at the fudge shop. I learned to love the flea market. So the next idea was super. Happiness finally was coming on to me. I would rent a space indoors with my military wares. They were only opened on weekends and closed in the winter. I was so excited.

My first spot was small and trying. My neighbors were watching, worried I was going to sell something that they were. No one was selling military. Good for me. That first year, I lost a little bit. Everyone told me it takes three years to get ahead. I was not happy with my results but did not care because I loved it. People from the store would come down and see what I was selling. I think they thought I was stealing it from the store. I already knew my own companies from the twenty-five years of dealing with them, so that was not true.

The next year I moved my spot over to where I had an outdoor porch, along with the indoor part, at a cheaper price even. That year was fantastic. I had my customer base and new ones as well. I had people from the store come to my spot just to see me. I made so much money that I had to purchase more and more inventory. I was happy, and right there, in the middle of my spot, was an eight-by-ten picture of the owner who was sadly missed. People commented on it all the time. My neighbors were getting closer to me also. Two other people there had the same kind of cancer I did. We actually had treatments together but did not know it. That was weird but a sign of something.

As time went by, the store was getting closer and closer to closing. I would hear rumors about moods and anger. I kept checking the probate.

One day it happened. It was around March of the sixth year when I heard the owner's house was going to be sold. I went online to see the listing for it. There were pictures of the inside, all messy, and then the bedroom where the bed was still had not been made up since the night he died. I gasped and right away called the realtor and angrily told how disrespectful and rude it was to post that. She said someone else did that, and she would take the bedroom one away.

The house sold but not without a hitch.

It seemed as though part of the land it was on was forgotten to go with the sale. So now more problems. The warehouse man was told to go clean the house all the way out now because it sold. The doctor did nothing to help on this and told them to throw it in a warehouse until further use. A lot of the items were very old Jewish ones. The warehouse man had had enough but still did as he wished.

I checked the probate record, and it said newly found assets. It had said this on and off a few times during the years. I don't know if it were items the doctor gave back or the fact they did not sell all the land to the new homeowner.

Come April of that year, I checked the records again. This time it listed the beneficiary in it. This was the first time in seven years it had said anything about them. Oh no, the sleeping dog must have woken up! I still feel bad about not contacting them but did not want to get killed by a hit man.

The beneficiary was not happy by the way it sounded. The bank was brought in because they were the trustee to the will. That's when I learned the workers' paychecks were now going to be signed by the bank, not by the coexecutor, the doctor.

May came next, the settlement entry filed by the lawyer was denied. Imagine that now, when they all knew they might be in a little jam. Squirming, I am sure.

June brought more beneficiaries into the picture.

August, they tried to have a settlement entry again, and it was denied.

After this settlement entry was denied, it read the judge called a sponte. I looked it up, and he threw everything and everyone out.

It was said the beneficiary was not allowed to have been running a business since it is a museum. Things needed to move fast so they kicked them all out. I only hoped they did not receive any money for this bad situation and all these years that had passed. They deserved jail time if I had my way.

The doctor came in September to the store and told them he would no longer be coming to visit. I was so happy to hear this.

The trust set up meetings for closing the stores. The letter read as follows:

As you may know, the owner's estate will soon be closing, and the ownership of the stores will be transferring to the owner's trust, which is the bank. Please plan on attending a meeting on September 6 at the store. Representatives of the trust will be on hand to answer questions.

I visited the store a lot in the final days. I wanted to see Vern and the store. I wanted to see how everyone was feeling, and they were sad. That made me mad because they created this monster and did nothing to help the situation.

November came and with it another letter. The bank was going to auction the stores off. My heart hurt every time I heard the latest. I had to drive by the store every day I went into town. I tried not to look over, but that never worked.

November 22: To the employees

As you know, we have been advertising the sale of the assets of the stores through an auction on December 5 and 6. We have agreed to sell all the real estate.

We are in contract to sell the real estate. Unfortunately, the investor has informed us that he does not intend to continue to run the stores.

We are also in contract to sell the south store to the accountant. The good news is that he intends to continue to operate the store and will interview current employees.

The remainder of the inventory will be auctioned off December 5.

The last day of operation of the stores will be November 27, 2017.

We want to thank you for all your hard work and dedication through this unsettled time. The owner would be proud of your efforts.

Sincerely,

The trust

It now was making sense why the inventory would always be off and the financial statements not right. The accountant was going to have his family run the south store.

Two weeks before the store was closing, a big order of outdoor jackets, bibs, jeans, hats, gloves, socks, you name it, came in.

"That was weird," said a friend of mine who was still working at the store.

They never unpacked it. It just set in the warehouse until one day when it all got shipped to the south store. Crooked, crooked, crooked—what a great way to set up your new store.

I actually called the auctioneers and told them what was happening. They seemed to care less. I then realized they were in on it too.

The newspaper advertised the auction, so the stores became very busy.

I was planning on going to the auction. How very hard it would be. I needed to speak my mind to the accountant once and for all.

I visited the store one final time at night to see Vern and to take a last look around. Now there was this eye doctor the owner went to about an hour away, and I got to know him. His family pictures were on his wall, and I often commented on them. I heard his son was a doctor now and had come to our town to practice. I had never met him, only saw him as a younger man on this wall.

That night in the store, a man came in and looked around.

I said, "Do you need some help?" just like I still worked there.

He looked at Vern who was sitting in a chair and said, "You look familiar. Oh, you are just blending in with the wall."

We did not know what he meant, but the riddle told me he was Jewish as he well looked it. He walked away into the store. He looked around, and then it hit me: This is the eye doctor's son. Never had I met him before, but I just knew he was, and the owner sent him to me.

I asked the man if he was a doctor. He said, "My nurse thinks so."

I laughed and said, "Does your last name begin with a K?" He said I found him out, and then I explained who I was. He said no one drove the owner, and I said, "I did to your father for macular disease."

He said, "Oh, you are right."

I said, "Your picture is on his wall." He said yes and was so sad to see this place go. I said, "Don't blame me. I left three years ago." He said the owner left it to the Holocaust Museum. I said yes but what a bad mess it became. I told him to tell his father hello.

That was so strange, but I knew who did that. Vern could not believe I figured this man out.

The next time I went to the store would be the final time. The auction was supposed to be fast. I am pretty sure it was not a good auction because people were not happy about the way it was done. I needed a T-shirt rack.

I went in to the stores trying not to shed a tear. Everything were in lots. I saw a lot of people I knew. I went and got a ticket and was not very friendly to anyone. The auctioneer wore a big cowboy hat. He was an idiot. The auction was to start in my store. I did not stand a chance on making a bid for my flea market shop. The auctioneer yelled it so fast, and big buyers grabbed each lot before I even got a chance to see where they were even at on lots. I did get to bid on one lot but got outbid. The only thing I got at a great price was a huge box of P38s.

We all went over to the big store for the next part. I walked in, and there he was, the crooked accountant. I wondered if he ever felt guilty about receiving merchandise at his new south store before the auction from the back warehouse. We were at the knives and showcases when he made eye contact with me. His sons were with him, I am assuming the ones who would be working at Daddy's new store.

He said to me in an unfriendly way, "Hey, Pam, how are you?" not even looking at me.

I said, "What the hell do you care?"

He said, "What is that supposed to mean?"

I said, "You got everything you wanted out of this and were very bad on your financial statements and, in my eyes, nothing but a crook."

He said, "That is bullshit," and I said, "Would you like to go over them with me and my husband one last time?"

His son looked shock and said to me, "You are nothing but filth."

I said, "You will know about your daddy someday." I then walked away about to punch them.

I left not long after that as I was not feeling well at all. I saw a man loading up his truck next door at my store. I really needed a T-shirt rack. So I yelled to him up in the truck, "Do you have a T-shirt rack you could sell me?" He said yes and gave me his card to call him.

I called him about a month later. He was not too far from me. He had a business that sold things and used the web a lot. He made T-shirts and decals for fishing products and racing. He told me to come up to his store and see what I liked. This man was amazing.

He looked like Richard Dreyfuss. He was so nice. He was Jewish but did not practice it much. Turned out, his grandmother went to the same synagogue as the owner. He knew all about the owner. I felt a real connection with him. Did the owner send me here? The owner and his grandmother knew each other.

It made me feel better talking to him about the whole situation of what happened to the store. He also was a cancer survivor like me. We were about the same age. This man suggested things I should carry at my shop. He made me decals and wonderful signs to try. They sold very fast at the shop.

He had designed my own T-shirt and sign for my shop. I am so glad I found this man.

My visits to the cemetery to see the owner are still ongoing. The sad part is that I don't think anyone visits him. Being so well-known and having so much money surprised me on this. I had made him some dog tags and laid them on the bottom of the headstone, along with my special shell and rock.

I would clean the stone every time I went. Sure enough, my dog tags would always be on the ground in the mud. I would get so mad. All I could imagine was the doctor doing this. I truly think it happens when they run the weed whacker in the summertime. I only hope that was it.

One day, as I was cleaning the stone, I noticed on the one side of it where his numbers are from all the camps he was in was fading out bad. I could not even read some of them. This bothered me. I went to where he bought this stone, knowing he had fought with these people, and showed them the picture I had taken of the fading numbers. I asked if they could engrave or make them brighter somehow. After all, these were very important numbers from very bad past. They said yes, they would get out there and do that. It has been one year, and I am still waiting.

I asked Vern the other day if he remembered any good stories about this amazing man whom he would like to add. He came up with a few. One was when he and a coworker were taking a break outside—in other words having a smoke—and the owner had already left for the day break. They were chatting it up with their ciggies when, lo and behold, the owner came around the corner with his car. He pulled up and gave them that look like no other could give, rolled down the window, and asked, "Are you enjoying yourselves? Smoking on my time?"

They just nodded and put them out and said, "Have a good night," and went back in the store. They could not help but giggle about this because they knew the owner was once a chain-smoker and had a heart attack because of chain-smoking. He would light two at once.

There was this area in front of the stores where truck drivers would love to turn around in. They tore up the pavement badly doing this. One day the owner was coming around in his car and caught a semitruck doing just this. He started blaring his horn and blocked the driver. He got out of his car and stood there staring at this trucker. The trucker stared back for five minutes and then slowly tried to back his way out. It was a hard position to do. The owner won this one.

The owner would overspend a little too much on auctions. We would have gotten in trouble for this. He must have had ten thousand sextants, paddles, face shields, wiring, etc.

He would manage to hit our front porch pole a few times to our building. We would hear this thud and knew he had arrived.

He came in one day and told Vern and I that any kind of bag we had, it needed to be stuffed. We tried to tell him we had many different types of bags, new and surplus ones. He said, "Great, now get stuffing." We thought he was being a bit difficult with this new job. He did not like the way we did it. "Make them puffier," he would say. We worked on all twelve of them for a week. Then he said, "Now display them properly along the wall." Oh, what a pain this was. But guess what? We sold more bags than ever and knew we were the dummies. Even to this day, I stuff my bags at my shop, thinking of him always.

As I was driving past the stores, they have become very beautiful. A lot of money had been put into them.

My son's thirtieth birthday came last year, and we all went to dinner. My sons started talking about the store and what a great experience it was to work there! I was shocked. They said they were so glad they worked there, and it was the best days.

That made me feel so good to hear that.

The store's billboard across the city was always all roads lead to the store. Now it would have to say led.

I have dreams about the owner all the time, some good, some bad. The best one was the night before I was to go to work at the flea market. He come into the store, and I had a customer who was buying hundreds of hat pins. The owner looked at me and smiled then shrugged and left.

The next day at work, my best seller was hat pins. I think I sold at least thirty. I have never sold that many. I hope he visits me again soon in my dreams.

The store is going to be an indoor craft mall. It looks wonderful. It is still very hard to look over there when I drive by. I have a new flea market spot. It is two times bigger and with three doors, with an L-shaped front porch. Hopefully, I will do well. This will be my fourth year there. Last year was the best, and I knew I needed to expand. I have made many good friends there. I love it.

Well, I gave a little bit. I gave a little of my time and life, and boy, did I get a lot.

He taught me a lot about history, business, and life itself.

And now my question to you is, when are you coming back?

I know the answer, but I also know he is with me on this venture.

CPSIA information can be obtained
at www.ICGtesting.com
Printed in the USA
BVHW081104110319
542311BV00012B/320/P

9 781490 794037